All the Other Things
I Really Need to Know
I Learned from Watching
STAR TREK:
THE NEXT GENERATION®

All the Other Things
I Really Need to Know
I Learned from Watching
STAR TREK:
THE NEXT GENERATION®

Dave Marinaccio

POCKET
BOOKS

NEW YORK   LONDON   TORONTO   SYDNEY   TOKYO   SINGAPORE

for Leslie,

and in memory of the Hartford Whalers

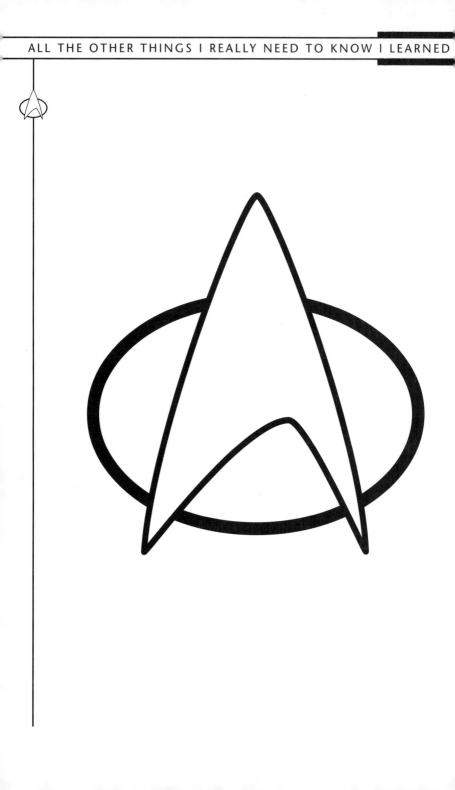

INTRODUCTION

C all me Dave Marinaccio. It's not as catchy as Ishmael, but I too have taken a journey. Well, not so much taken a journey as been taken on one. You see, I've never left my great white couch.

Captain Jean-Luc Picard of the *Starship Enterprise* NCC-1701-D visits me several nights a week in my living room. He does most of the talking. This doesn't mean the relationship is one-sided. I find Picard a most engaging fellow, and I've learned a great bit by residing in his presence.

He's not perfect. For starters, he's a fictional character. Of course, I've met many of those in my chosen occupation, advertising. In truth, Jean-Luc has more real substance than many of my professional brethren.

He's bad for my eyes when I watch him in the dark. And he must bear some of the burden for my expanding waistline and softening sofa springs. Still, when all is said and done, he's expanded my imagination at least as much as my belt size.

"But Dave, *Star Trek* is just a television show." I've heard that phrase a lot over the past couple of years. Ever since I wrote *All I Really Need to Know I Learned from Watching Star Trek*.

As a society we are hypnotized by television. The average American TV set is switched on over six hours a day. More people believe television news than believe newspapers. That little electronic box in our living rooms, dining rooms, dens, bedrooms, attics, basements, garages, kitchens, and bathrooms has changed the way we live. But when I dared to suggest that there is actually something to be learned from watching the tube, people looked at me as if I were from space.

Learn something from TV? You must be nuts. Why don't you go read a book? Books contain knowledge. Television is a vast wasteland, an idiot box, the boob tube. Incredibly, even hosts of television talk shows jabbed fun at the notion that I had found something of value on TV. Go figure.

If they're right, if there's nothing to be learned from TV, then I'm toast. I'm glued to that sucker. It takes me two turns to get home at night. First I turn the doorknob and then I turn on the set. Even when I'm not watching, it stays on. It's on now. I don't like to turn my back on it but I've got it trained. Me and my Zenith.

More to the point, I would like to suggest that the medium is *not* the message, and we shouldn't, like Elvis, shoot the messenger. Television is a conduit. It's neither better nor worse than other forms of communication.

What's being conveyed is what's truly important. The source of ideas is not as important as the substance of the ideas being expressed. Pretty heavy stuff, huh?

How about this? Ask yourself a simple question. Where do you think you will be exposed to more elevated ideas, in a television show written by Gene Roddenberry or in a book written by Fabio? Romance-novel fans should note that this a rhetorical question.

Watch any *Star Trek* or *Star Trek: The Next Generation* episode (or movie, or successive television spin-off), and you will visit a universe filled with ideas and lessons you can use in everyday life. Really. The most important of which is that someday the human race will actually like itself. Look at the bridge of the *Enterprise*-D. This is virtually the only show on television where all the major characters are good. They all treat each other with decency and respect. And—hold on to your seats—everyone gains from the experience.

Taking this idea a step further, they even try to treat the alien species they encounter in the same high-minded manner. This concept is so worthwhile, so noble, I can deal with a few latex alien creatures wearing silly noses and ears.

Other lessons cover the gamut of life on earth, like:

- It's OK to wear a beard to work.
- How to design a logo.
- The importance of exercise.
- How to tell twins apart. (If you don't know

how, an evil twin can confuse you into thinking he's—I mean "he is"—the good twin and feed you to a Crystalline Entity.)

And there's plenty more where those came from.

So I invite Picard into my living room. He brings along Riker and Troi and Data and Q. They're all welcome. So are Sisko and Janeway and Kirk. It can get crowded in here.

Yeah, I know *Star Trek* is just a TV show...just a well-written, imaginatively conceived, wonderfully entertaining television show with a strong morally centered philosophy that has so far spawned *The Original Series*, *The Next Generation*, *Star Trek: Deep Space Nine*, *Star Trek: Voyager*, a cartoon series, eight movies, countless novels, technical manuals, and a convention phenomenon thrown in for good measure.

In the next few pages I'll share some of the things I've discovered watching *The Next Generation*. Yes, I mean some of the things I've learned. There's a lot there. Maybe even everything you really need to know. Perhaps even enough to live long and prosper.

PICARD

O h Captain, my Captain. Even in the 24th century they can't find a cure for that pesky baldness chromosome. In some ways, Picard's well-buffed dome is the counterpoint to Kirk's less-than-ripped abdominals. You know, the humanizing imperfection that is less important than how the captain conducts himself.

Not that baldness is a physical shortcoming. It's the hairstyle of choice for some pretty attractive men. Perhaps Picard is the Michael Jordan of his generation. Then again, it's hard to imagine Jean-Luc hanging out with Dennis Rodman.

More to the point, there are many things to be learned from watching Jean-Luc. Principally because Picard is so well-rounded as a person. Sure he's a great starship captain. By some folks' reckoning, he's the best starship captain. But there's a whole lot more to this flying Frenchman.

He's a musician. OK, so he learned to play his instrument in a coma while living an alternate life courtesy of an alien space probe. That may be a little weird, but it's certainly not any stranger than stories I've heard from other musicians I know. And to the captain's credit he continues to practice his flute. (Or whatever that flute-type thing is.)

The commander of the *U.S.S. Enterprise* NCC-1701-D, Captain Jean-Luc Picard (Patrick Stewart).

Picard is also a trained and practicing archaeologist. So the space explorer keeps his feet firmly on the ground and in the substrata. It is more than just an academic pursuit; Jean-Luc shows a curiosity and respect for things that happened long before he roamed the galaxy.

He's an animal lover and an equestrian, and he even keeps his own saddle on the *Enterprise*-D (which probably hints at a strong attraction to leather as well—but never mind).

He exercises vigorously, sometimes by playing a futuristic version of racquetball; on other occasions he enjoys a more ancient form of physical recreation, fencing (this proves you can be well-rounded and still have a sharp point).

Ultimately, Picard is an explorer. It's more than his job; it's the way he approaches life. I hope I share that with the captain. I'd love to sit at the helm of a vessel of exploration. Unfortunately, I don't have the opportunity to command the *Enterprise*.

Instead, my voyages of discovery take place right here on terra firma. I try to learn or do one new thing every year. I took up skydiving one year. Another I studied astronomy at the Adler Planetarium in Chicago. I even took break-dancing lessons. I now have an intimate understanding of where the term "break" dancing came from.

Some of these experiences have become lifelong activities. Others, mercifully, were never repeated. But all of them have made my life fuller. I've also come to realize that I only experienced them because of a conscious decision to pursue them.

Hey, the universe doesn't come to the captain of the *Enterprise*-D. He must "seek out" new life and new experiences. His intelligence, curiosity, and imagination drive him. And they remind us that what's in your head is more important than what's on it.

Shortly after my first book was published, my alma mater invited me back to speak. It had been a long time since I drove the winding roads of eastern Connecticut. I enjoyed the trip as I headed into the little valley where the school is located. On the left is a sheep farm, at the bottom of the hill is a church, and as I neared the right-hand turn for the bookstore I motored under a banner.

Giant letters proclaimed, "Welcome to the University of Connecticut, the best years of your life." A small smile crossed my lips as I recalled some of the good times at UConn: shoots on Thursday nights, short skirts, basketball games, entertaining professors, war protests.

Then I started to think. I was having a pretty good year; I'd traveled, had a book published, met new people, owned a home, drove a sports car, made good money, and was looking forward to lots more. The year I was living was far better than any I experienced in college. What were they implying? That it's all downhill after college, that those are the best years? Just hold on a second, buddy. If I thought college was the best part of my life, I would have committed suicide a long time ago. Get some perspective. College was fun, but whoever put up that banner should be tested for brain damage.

Every year is a new opportunity for the best year of your life. Every year is an opportunity to explore strange new worlds, to seek out new life and new experiences. To boldly go where you have never gone before.

I like to believe I've embraced that philosophy as my own. That it is an attitude.

I also like a subtle change made in the wording of this paraphrased statement. (Not the change I just made.) When Picard reads the mission statement at the beginning of *The Next Generation,* he doesn't talk about a five-year mission as Kirk did on *The Original Series.* He calls the *Enterprise*'s voyage a "continuing mission."

My college career was a five-year mission. It wasn't supposed to be. It just took me a little longer than my contemporaries to get the required number of credits. So, in a way, I had a head start on lengthening my exploration into a continuing education.

I've heard it said, "Life is just one damn thing after another." And that is true. The future will show up at your door whether you want it to or not.

In *Star Trek Generations,* we saw how two men confronted the next damn thing. Malcolm McDowell, playing the evil and demented Dr. Soran, wanted to stop the future...to go back to an idyllic time of family life that had passed. He saw time as a stalking predator that would "hunt you down and make the kill."

Jean-Luc Picard saw time a different way. "Time is a

Dr. Tolian Soran (Malcolm McDowell) and Picard: two men with opposing philosophical beliefs about the role of Time in their lives.

companion who goes with us on the journey and reminds us to cherish every moment." Picard looked forward to the next damn thing, anticipated it, reveled in it. No doubt waiting to explore it—boldly.

I think if I could have gotten a ladder tall enough, Jean-Luc would have helped me rip down that banner at my alma mater. And then we would have proceeded smartly to the next thing, the best damn year of our lives.

Amber and T.J. are as opposite as any four-year-olds can be. Amber is a girl. Timothy John is a boy. She's blond. He's dark. She's quiet. He doesn't shut up. About the only thing they have in common is their birthday. They're twins.

They're also my niece and nephew. While playing with them the other day, I discovered another thing they have in common, their choice of toys. Both were playing with small replicas of the Mighty Morphin Power Rangers. From what I gather, the chief attraction of the Power Rangers is that they kick. Most of the time was spent with the figures kicking each other, with an occasional foot aimed at Uncle Dave.

The kick-a-thon was progressing quite nicely until a word escaped from my young niece's lips. Amber called her Power Ranger a "doll." T.J. reacted so violently to this that he actually stopped fighting. A guttural yell exploded from his diaphragm.

I should note at this point that T.J. doesn't talk—he yells. But this wasn't his normal yelling. It was a scream of righteous indignation.

"They're not dolls. They're action figures." The male twin looked directly at me. "Right?" he demanded.

Now both pairs of eyes were trained on wise Uncle Dave. I felt like Jean-Luc Picard when he was chosen Arbiter of Succession of the Klingon Empire in the "Reunion" episode. The Klingons were engaged in a nasty fight about who would ascend to the leadership of the Klingon High Council. Both Duras and Gowron had legitimate claims. Suddenly and unexpectedly, Picard found himself in the middle. He would have to decide which claim was correct. Even though Picard was no authority on Klingon law or custom.

Picard's path would guide me here. First, the captain of the *Enterprise*-D asked Duras and Gowron each to tell of his qualifications for such a high position.

So I, in turn, asked Amber and T.J. why they held the opinions they did (I used simpler language). Amber thought the Power Rangers were dolls because they looked exactly like her other dolls. T.J. thought the Power Rangers were action figures because that's what the TV commercials called them.

As an unscrupulous adman I should have sided with T.J., but I couldn't. I had a higher calling. I was Uncle Arbiter. Besides, there wasn't a real answer. The toys actually met the definition for dolls. Years ago my Madison Avenue brethren decided that parents wouldn't buy dolls for their male offspring, so they created a new name for boys' dolls: action figures.

That's right, kids, I could have said, society is so frightened a boy might play with a doll that we make up fake words. You must be properly sex-role stereotyped. You must conform to societal norms. You will be assimilated. Resistance is futile. Otherwise we can't be held responsible when, after puberty, you end up in therapy.

Finally, it came to me. Picard's primary motivation was to buy time so he could figure out a way to prevent a Klingon civil war. In Picard's case the problem solved itself when the leader of one of the Klingon factions was killed.

Hey, I thought, the kids can worry about sex-role stereotyping when they take sociology in college. The key here was to avert bloodshed, to buy time.

Looking at my niece, I knew what I had to do. "Amber," I said slowly, "your Power Ranger is yellow. The yellow ones are dolls. So are the pink ones." No fool I. I knew that the yellow and pink Power Rangers were girls. This answer seemed to satisfy Amber.

Next I trained my gaze on T.J. "Your Power Ranger is red," I articulated, "and the red Power Rangers are action figures."

This seemed to satisfy both, and the kicking happily resumed.

On *The Original Series,* Captain Kirk always chose himself to lead the "landing party." On *The Next Generation,* Picard usually remains on the ship after assigning Riker to lead an "away team." This seems appropriate for Jean-Luc. After all, he's definitely not a "party" guy.

It also clearly shows what kind of manager Picard is.

He's a delegator—a very unusual delegator, a successful one. The folks he chooses to accomplish tasks usually succeed. There's much to be learned from this.

My dad used this management technique when I was growing up. He would delegate tasks to me. "David, pick that up," he would say, as we both gazed upon some object on the living-room floor that was certainly dropped by my brother Mark. At this point, all similarity between my dad and Jean-Luc ended.

"I didn't put it there," I would shoot back.

"I don't care who put it there. I want you to pick it up," Dad would retort.

"Get Mark to pick it up," I would suggest.

"David, if you don't pick that up I'm going to hit you with the yardstick."

This is one of my father's threats I always took seriously. My father handled a yardstick with the skill a blind man shows at archery. He was all over the place, and the innocent were hit as often as his intended target. All in all, not a pretty sight.

By then, neither was my dad. His face was swollen and the color of a sunset that delights sailors. His body was like a coil ready to snap. In this situation there was only one response. No, not pick up the object. *Run!* Run like the wind.

Let me tell you something. My dad was thirty-five when I was born. If he had been in his twenties, those few years' difference might have given him enough speed and energy to catch me. As it was, I could usually elude him and disappear until he calmed down or forgot the event altogether.

If I stayed away long enough, the stuff lying around on the floor would be gone by the time I returned. The house would be quiet. It would be as if I'd gone into a time warp and prevented the event from occurring.

What was I talking about? Oh yeah, Picard the delegator. I believe the reason Picard is so successful with this management style is that he clearly defines everyone's role. Sometimes the roles are already assigned. Obviously it's Dr. Crusher's duty to discover the cause of a medical problem. Sometimes though, it's not as cut and sutured. In those circumstances, Picard gathers everyone in the conference room, listens to their analyses and suggestions, then assigns roles.

Courses of action are also talked about, but the individuals have great latitude to improvise. In "The Ensigns of Command," Picard assigns various tasks to different crew members. La Forge and O'Brien must devise a way to make the transporter work through the interference of hyperonic radiation. Troi assists Picard in finding loopholes in the treaty with the Sheliak. Data is sent to prepare colonists to abandon their settlement. Simple. A job for everyone and everybody goes to work.

Better yet: In "Redemption, Part II," Picard delegates the command of a ship to Data. During his command, Data disobeys a direct order from Picard in order to take a decisive action. When Picard summons the android to his ready room, Data is prepared for a court martial. Instead Picard supports the actions of his lieutenant commander.

Why? Because as much as I love my dad, Picard is a better manager. He knows that a successful delegator doesn't delegate tasks, he delegates authority. And when you give people authority, it's theirs to use as they see fit. Your job is to support them. Picard does.

My friend Jim Vec and his girlfriend are having a fight. That's fine. Most relationships have some edge to them. Besides, Jim—like myself—is an Italian, so we consider fighting normal. Donna, his friend, isn't as comfortable with this concept.

Before I go on I'd like to comment on something. I have three good friends named Jim. You can also toss an Uncle Jim into the mix. Actually Uncle Jim's real name is Oswaldo, so naturally he goes by his second name, James, which condenses to Jim. This makes more sense than using his initials and calling himself O.J. Marinaccio.

So I'm surrounded by all these Jims. Not to be confused with a gym, which seldom surrounds me.

Anyhow, is this a common name? There's only one on *Star Trek*. Never mind.

But I was talking about fighting as part of a relationship. A lot has been written about it. Stuff that says fighting is OK if—big *if*—it's fair fighting. Some say small fights defuse bigger fights, like Vesuvius letting off steam rather than exploding. The bulk of the literature agrees with Jim and me that fighting is healthy.

Star Trek concurs. Keiko and Miles have their ups and downs. So do Riker and Troi. The exception is Picard. The majority of times we've seen the captain in a relationship, he's been a perfect gentleman. Never so much as raises his voice. He gets a little irritated with Dr. Crusher from time to time, but who wouldn't? As Q says, she gets more shrill with each passing year. In "True Q" she got far enough under Q's hide to have the omnipotent one turn her into a dog. Of course, Picard would never do that.

Too bad. Not that the captain should turn the doctor into an Irish setter. But it's too bad Picard never shows the passion to his future wife (according to "All Good Things...") that he shows toward that virtual outlaw Vash.

This demonstrates the obvious. Picard is crazy about Vash. They fight so fiercely that Q once teased them, saying they were acting like a married couple. Interesting observation, don't you think?

Hey, love is a strong emotion. Let a strong emotion loose and other powerful emotions are sure to follow.

That's what my friends Vec and Donna are experiencing.

I believe in the old expression that says, when you meet someone you really like there are sparks. The sparks are easy to see with Vec and Donna, just as with Jean-Luc and Vash. The same sparks are bound to set off an explosion or two. In a circumstance like that there's only one thing to do: enjoy the fireworks.

At a restaurant the other night, my dinner companion uttered a phrase I've heard many times. "The fish is fishy."

I'm not sure why this set me off. But it did. Of course, the fish is fishy! What else could the fish be? Nobody complains the steak is steaky. The chicken is chickeny. The wine is winey. If you don't want something fishy, then don't order the fish. Hell, yes, the fish is fishy!

Still, my friend insisted and called the waitress. After a brief smell the waitress agreed.

Now it was two against one. I pointed out that if the fish weren't fishy, *that* would be a reason to complain. In fact, if the latter were the case, there should be an investigation. The reason the fish is fishy is because—

figure it out—it's fish! What is fish supposed to taste like? Kumquats?

The waitress quickly removed the offensive fishy-tasting fish, effectively ending our absurd discussion. It also turned into my last evening out with my fish-eating companion.

In retrospect, maybe I didn't really handle that situation all that well. What people are saying and what they mean are often two completely different things. This is a concept that has been explored on *Star Trek* many times, never better than with that crazy-looking pigman alien, Dathon, from the episode "Darmok."

Picard and crew are warping through space exploring strange new worlds when they meet up with a spaceship of the Children of Tama. This species and humans have met before but have never been able to communicate with each other. Each can understand the words the other race speaks but not the meaning behind them.

The *Enterprise* would send a message that says something like, "Hey, how you guys doing over there?" Then the Children of Tama would reply, "The fish is fishy." These exchanges got them absolutely nowhere. Worse still, there was no waitress to call over to serve as referee.

In desperation, Dathon kidnaps Picard and forces him to go camping. (No, really, this is what happened.) On the camping trip, the local equivalent of a giant grizzly bear shows up and tries to eat them.

Forced to work together, Picard and Dathon devise a

strategy enabling them to fight the bear. This bear-type thing isn't easy to describe. It looked like a large version of an old-time electric logo called Reddy Kilowatt—which I'm sure no one under forty years old remembers. For those not of my demographic, pick any mutant X-Man, use only his outline, and pretend the show is in black and white.

As the experience of Dathon (Paul Winfield) and Picard illustrates, sometimes true understanding comes only through a shared experience.

Robbie Robinson

Eventually, Picard realizes that Dathon is speaking in metaphors. He is citing examples from the past, which is great, but the examples he is using come from the history of the Children of Tama. Picard still can't relate.

When the bear/Reddy Kilowatt/X-Man shows up, Picard and Dathon put their plan into effect. As they do, the *Enterprise* tries to beam Picard off the camping planet. Frozen in the transporter beam, Picard watches helplessly as the bear gets Dathon and kills him.

Now Picard has some serious explaining to do to the Children of Tama. Luckily the experience he has just been through allows him to use a few simple metaphors, enough to communicate with the grieving crew aboard the alien vessel. This time they see the meaning in his words and understand.

Picard accomplished what I had failed to do at that restaurant. He looked for and found the meaning in their words rather than getting hung up on the semantics of their statements. What a person means is more important then how it's said. It's a lesson that, over the years, I've come to appreciate. Along with another subtle maxim. Sometimes the fish really does taste fishy.

RIKER

*T*he other night I was thinking about Commander Riker's beard and Walt Disney's mustache. They both look great. For someone who hates to shave as much as I do, the thought made me very envious.

I did have a beard and mustache, once, in the seventies. Shaving the beard left me with a small brown caterpillar on my lip that was the fashion in those days. It wasn't very good looking; scraggly and thin would have been a generous description. Worse still, the seventies were the disco era.

As I headed out the door on many a Saturday night in my patterned rayon shirt and platform shoes, I cut quite a bizarre figure. Mercifully there are few photographs of me from that period.

So anyway, I heard Jonathan Frakes (aka Commander Riker) tell the story about his beard. He too hates shaving. So between the first two seasons of *The Next Generation*, he let his follicles grow. As the cast readied to resume production, he showed his whiskers to Gene Roddenberry.

Roddenberry had no objection to Riker's new look. He figured the men who went to sea grew beards, why shouldn't the men who go into space? "We'll make it a nautical beard," is how Frakes said Roddenberry stated it.

The first officer of the *Enterprise*-D, Commander William T. Riker (Jonathan Frakes).

Elliott Marks

Great, Dave, but what on God's green earth does that have to do with Walt Disney?

Everything. Well, actually it says more about Disney Corporation than it does about the son of Elias and Flora Disney. You see, Walt grew a mustache as a way to look older during his early years in Hollywood. As a young entrepreneur, he felt the facial hair would help him look more mature. He and the other animators in his fledgling shop all grew mustaches on a bet. Walt kept his 'stache the rest of his life.

Now get this. Employees at Disney World are not allowed to have facial hair. Grow a mustache and you lose your job. No exceptions. Which means if young Walt Disney applied for a job at Disney World, he'd be turned away. Forget it buddy. We don't want your kind around here.

Talk about forgetting your roots. *Wow!*

Here's a little fantasy for you. Suppose that Walt Disney's mustache actually made him look more mature. Suppose that his more mature look increased Walt's self-confidence. Suppose that confidence was the major ingredient for his success. Ergo a mustache is responsible for the entire Disney empire—it's a multi-billion-dollar mustache.

Kind of makes you feel sorry for the silly bureaucrat who outlawed facial hair at Disney World.

Meanwhile, back at Riker's beard: contrast and compare. Gene Roddenberry saw a cast member assert his individuality and he supported it. Those who are different on *Star Trek* are accepted. Not only on the show but in reality as well.

Both Walt Disney and Gene Roddenberry are heroes of mine. Both have lasting legacies. Let's hope the people who now control the future of Gene Roddenberry's creation have more sense than their counterparts in Orlando.

No discussion of William Riker is complete without mention of his tremendous appetite for women. In fact, tremendous might not be a large enough word. What we're taking about here is the nonstop pursuit of the female of every species in the galaxy. He's more than a Casanova, he's a Casasupernova.

Hey, sex is healthy. None of us would be here without it. The propagation of the species is important. But…

Riker as the ladies' man: enviably passionate, admirably honest.

Back at the University of Connecticut I learned about Sigmund Freud, the Father of Psychology. Freud's basic idea was that virtually all human behavior was dictated by the sex drive. For most of us, there seems to be at least some validity in these theories. But now I realize the creator of psychoanalysis was specifically referring to Commander Riker.

Obviously William T.'s proclivities are easy to joke about. Let's just say the *Starship Enterprise* isn't the only thing with warp thrusters on it and let it end there.

What gets lost in all this talk of lusting is that Riker is emotionally very honest. He is driven by equal amounts of testosterone and truth.

His relationship with Deanna Troi is a case in point. Think back on your old flames. Can you still talk? Can you still share closeness? Can you let them go?

"All Good Things..." notwithstanding, Riker can. He doesn't love 'em and leave 'em. He chases women, and when he catches them, he makes friends.

I often think back on the women I didn't pursue. In retrospect a little Riker wouldn't have hurt. The commander never hesitates when he feels attraction. He leads with his heart.

Did I just say a little Riker wouldn't have hurt? In the real world, throwing your heart around can hurt— big time. In fact, you can get your heart run over by a tractor trailer. You can experience agony. Love is definitely not for the timid.

Men generally make the first move in romantic

liaisons. Traditionally, it's been our role to break the ice. Riker is fearless in this situation. But most of us aren't like Riker. For a guy like me, there's a lot of rejection involved. The pain I experience is real. Callous women have whacked some serious dents in the fenders of my self-image.

I remember walking across a crowded room to, I had hoped, kindle a conversation with a brunette who was sitting alone. On the way, I ran through a mental checklist of witty opening lines: "Pardon me, I believe I dropped my Nobel peace prize under your table." "If I said you had a beautiful body, would you hold it against me?" "Can I buy you a small home in the suburbs?"

I settled on saying "Hi." Ms. Brunette, who had watched my final few steps to her table, looked up at me. "Can't you see?" she scowled, "I'm talking with my friend."

Maybe. Maybe she was. Maybe her friend was in the ladies' room powdering her nose. Maybe her friend had engaged a cloaking device. Absolutely, she made me feel like an idiot.

Granted, this is an extreme example, but every time a man approaches a woman he faces this humiliating possibility. Some women are more gentle; some are a lot worse. It's why I admire Riker's nerve.

His approach does have rewards. You won't waste time deceiving yourself. You'll always know where you stand. And as Riker told Data in the episode "In Theory," when the android considered dating a shipmate, "When it really works between two people, it's like nothing you've ever experienced." Amen.

Lieutenant Commander Data (Brent Spiner) tries to understand relationships between men and women with the help of Lieutenant Jenna D'Sora (Michele Scarabelli).

Since I started this, we might as well continue. Men and women often seem as different as alien species. It's something that puzzles everyone over the age of thirteen (and frequently those younger). While I will not settle this issue in the next page or so, Commander Riker seems an appropriate place to entertain speculation.

In the lunchroom at work this very topic came up. A coworker had read an article about brain activity suggesting different genders used different areas of the brain. The implication of such a suggestion is that men and women perceive the world differently. That we are not only anatomically dissimilar, but also cognitively different.

Before you begin to think that our lunchroom is a foundation think tank, let me introduce you to some of the other serious questions we have discussed. *Can a baby burp while it's still in the womb? How many heads did the Highlander lop off last week? Why do the family photographs of a colleague always reveal her dog's rear end?* You know, the real important issues in life.

Anyhow, we jumped into this "Do males and females think differently?" thing. The conversation was brilliant: "Yes." "No." "No way." "Way." "Maybe." In short, the whole conversation was more boring than dialogue from *thirtysomething* and sputtered to an end.

Suddenly I remembered *Star Trek IV: The Voyage Home.* To pass time on their time trip into the past, McCoy approached Spock. "You really have gone where no man has gone before," began the doctor. McCoy was referring to the fact that Spock had died and been resurrected.

Spock, sitting calmly at his station in the captured Klingon bird-of-prey, paused. "It would be impossible to discuss the subject without a common frame of reference." Obviously dissatisfied, McCoy glared at the once-dead Vulcan. "You mean I have to die to discuss your insights on death?" And that, for all practical purposes, ended the conversation.

So too, in the lunchroom. The amazing thing about *Star Trek* is that everyone understood exactly what I was saying. Of course, in the lunchroom they're used to my comparisons to *Star Trek*.

The point is simple. Until we learn to read minds, men and women will never know if we think the same or differently.

It could be the thought processes of men and women are similar, along the lines of Coke and Pepsi. Or we could be as different as Coke and carpet tacks. There's really no way to tell. As Spock says, we don't have a common frame of reference.

In fact, no one knows if any two same-gender people think the same way, let alone if the sexes think differently. Even Dionne Warwick's closest friends don't have a clue.

We should keep trying to find out. Surely, exploring space includes exploring the space between our ears. In the meantime, we should just be thankful that we can sit in the lunchroom and enjoy each other's company.

Here's a dilemma. You can be promoted to the highest rank of your career. Have your choice of assignments. Achieve your lifelong ambition. Or you can stay second banana. What would you do?

What does Riker do? He slips on a peel. He chokes. He blows it. Let's get this straight—I like Riker. William T. has many admirable qualities. But he has refused command. Turns down the chance to sit in the big chair. Why? What were the writers drinking? Number One deserves better.

Hell, he is better. Judging by the objective evidence, Riker is a better captain than Picard. Check this out. In "The Best of Both Worlds," Picard is captured and assimilated by the Borg. He takes command of the Borg's big black Rubik's Cube. You know, that square block thing that the Borg call a spaceship.

So Riker and Picard face off. Mano a mano. The stakes, the future of humanity. Picard has a bigger ship, a faster ship, a more powerful ship, a ship that reacts as quickly as Picard has a thought, a ship that has gone through Starfleet like Chris Farley went through doughnuts. Locutus, Picard's new name as a Borg, has every conceivable advantage.

Riker on the other hand has a first officer, Shelby, who wants him dead. His side, the Federation, is apractic. And, of course, his opponent just happens to be the man who trained him.

So what does Riker do? He fakes to the left. He splits the *Enterprise*-D in two. He sends in a shuttlecraft and steals Locutus—Picard—right off the big black Rubik's Cube.

Picard had the superior ship. But Number One, true to his name, out-captained the captain. Riker beat Picard, TKO. Then he goes on to save the human race. Perhaps the entire galaxy. These are exploits up to Kirkian standards.

Riker as captain (flanked by Worf [Michael Dorn] and Troi [Marina Sirtis]): a man who fits perfectly in the command chair.

Robbie Robinson

In "A Matter of Honor," Riker is placed aboard a Klingon vessel. He learns their ways and becomes a valued crew member. When push comes to shove, as it often does on a Klingon bird-of-prey, Riker tricks the Klingon captain. He assumes command of the ship, puts the crew in its place, and forces the ship with which they are in potential combat to surrender. Oh, by the way, the captain of the ship that surrenders to Riker is Picard. This is getting to be a habit.

In the captain's chair—on either a Federation or Klingon vessel—Riker isn't just "number one"; he's undefeated. His methods are creative, resourceful, and unorthodox. After these experiences, there is no question where his proper place is. Starfleet knows it. As Shelby says after the Borg affair, "You can have the choice of any Starfleet command."

So what does Riker do? He declines promotion. He stays on the *Enterprise*-D as first officer, Number One, second in command.

I don't know about you, but this frustrates the heck out of me. I mean, c'mon, Riker, get a clue. Wake up and smell the *raktajino*. Cut the apron strings.

Listen, if you're ever in a comparable situation, do not follow William Thomas Riker's example. Go for it. Climb as high as you can go. Test yourself. Push until you find your boundaries. And enjoy yourself every step of the way. Because you'll never know what you can do until you do it.

I guess the thing that bothers me the most about Riker's refusal of promotion is that, I feel, he turned his back on his best destiny. I hope we see this talented commander in the captain's chair again. Maybe on *Deep Space Nine* or *Voyager*, or in a movie. Hey, that big chair is where he belongs.

DATA

*I*n 300 A.D. a group of people called the Teotihuacán built a city on a plain in central Mexico. They painted, sculpted, and built magnificent buildings—one reached the height of 21 stories. The population of this ancient metropolis was 125,000. This made Teotihuacán larger than another bustling town of the time, Rome.

Of course the citizens of Rome knew nothing of the North Americans. And the Teotihuacán were totally unaware that Rome ruled the world.

I stood on the Pyramid of the Moon and looked down the central avenue of that ancient Indian city. These people had every right to believe they were the preeminent civilization of all time.

I get the same feeling when I fly into New York. As the plane moves up the East River and I gaze to my left at Manhattan, the sight is awe-inspiring.

But there's a difference between me and the priests of Teotihuacán, aside from the flamboyant hats the Mexicans wore. I can never look at the Big Apple and believe it's the glory of the universe. Instead I imagine there's an intelligent being on another planet looking (or whatevering) at one of the wonders of its civilization, sharing the moment with me. And even though we haven't met yet, I'm sure he's (excuse the earthly chauvinism) as real as the Teotihuacán were during the days of Rome.

By the way, I don't mean to go overboard on this New York thing. I've spent a lot of time there, and as awe-inspiring as it can be, most of it isn't the flower of human culture. It's dirty, people stumble around talking to themselves, and the Mets stink. But every American city has problems.

Take L.A....please. The traffic is horrible, turning the air into smog. There's a tremendous gang and crime problem. Most of the time the residents live in a drought that amplifies seasonal firestorms. When it finally does rain, the precipitation causes mudslides. And, on occasion, earthquakes shake the entire city and buildings fall down. Still the people that live there love it.

Anyhow, what I'm getting around to is innocence and uniqueness. Stay with me. The Teotihuacán perceived themselves as unparalleled. I don't believe this was arrogance; there were just no others like them in their universe. They were also the most technologically advanced people in their frame of reference. Remind you of anyone?

Here's a hint. He is the most technologically advanced person in his frame of reference. And there are no others like him in the known universe. Yes, I'm talking about Data. (Forget the evil twin stuff for the time being.)

The android Lieutenant Commander Data: less than human...or more?

Data. So much power and so little arrogance. Funny thing: Data wants so badly to be human, but any human with Data's properties would probably be a very bad person. Arrogance would be the least of it. The more powerful people are, the less connected they seem to the rest of us. I mean, look what happened to Gary Mitchell in the second *Star Trek* pilot episode: zapped by an alien beam, he becomes godlike and tries to take over the ship with little regard for the inferiors who were formerly his crewmates. Look at Barclay in *The Next Generation:* zapped by an alien beam he becomes godlike and tries to take over the ship with little regard for the inferiors who were formerly his crewmates.

Wait a minute, Dave, are you trying to say *Star Trek* recycles scripts? Well, er, maybe it was just déjà vu.

The point is, give people a little power and they go nuts. Lottery winners freak out. Put a secretary in control of petty cash and suddenly she becomes King Midas. Want to turn a fifth grader into a despot? Just make him a hall monitor. Absolute power corrupts absolutely.

In many ways Data is the best *person* on the *Enterprise-D*. He's honest, humble, and caring. If you judge him by how he acts, he gives much to emulate. I'm glad he didn't attend St. Joseph's when I was a grade schooler. He would have been an impossible role model. The nuns would have sainted him.

This begs the question about Lieutenant Commander Android. Does he have a soul? Ahhh. Certainly not as much as Aretha Franklin, but he can dance. The real answer depends on your definition. If "soul" is the essence of who we are, he does have a soul, for he is very much his own individual.

As for the immortal report card where God keeps score, does Data have one of those? Is there a place in heaven for a souped-up Cuisinart? Who knows? These questions beget more questions than answers.

Data is simply living his life as a good and ethical person. If there's a lesson in this, it's that living a good life is its own reward. If more of us followed this example, it wouldn't matter what happens to Data's soul; we'd have a piece of heaven right here on Earth.

I dated Joan many years ago. She had a wonderful manner. A person who enjoyed living. Sometimes as we would walk, she would whistle.

I never could whistle. Still can't. But she had a small, pleasant whistle that came spontaneously.

As I became aware of the habit, I would join in. She would whistle. I would pass air over my teeth, producing a hissing sound. Usually Joan would laugh, and we would head on in silence.

Over time her whistle gradually disappeared. At first I was puzzled. A little reflection alerted me to the terrible truth. I had killed it.

See, she whistled without noticing it. It was as natural for Joan as swinging her arms when she walked. My hissing had brought her habit into her consciousness. Made her aware of what she was doing. Soon she would catch herself, realize she was whistling. And stop.

When this insight hit me, I felt terrible. I made a very conscious effort not to respond when Joan whistled. I stayed silent and let her whistle in peace. It took a little time, but eventually the little trill returned. And I remained quiet.

The same thing has happened to me. Once, I used *Star Trek* analogies to explain all that was explainable in life. It worked great. People understood my points and related to the analogies. It was clear, clean communication. People understood and then we moved on.

Then I wrote *All I Really Need to Know I Learned from Watching Star Trek*. After which a subtle change took place. It would occur any time I related a situation to *Star Trek*. People reacted in a way they never had before. A little "Aha."

I found this to be embarrassing, and I stopped using examples from *Star Trek*. It didn't end my career or anything. But I felt I had lost something, a way of expressing myself. And I thought of Joan.

Unfortunately, I was going to have to do this myself. I likened it to Data writing a subroutine for himself. When he encounters something new or wants to explore a part of his personality, he changes his programming to modify the way he responds.

I did the same thing. I forced myself to continue using the analogies and to ignore the "Ahas." Not an easy thing to do. But it worked.

Star Trek is still one of the best ways to illustrate a point. I will always use it. It's part of how I communicate. Part of me.

There's nothing wrong with change in life. Much of it is good. But make sure *you* pick. *You* decide. Keep the parts of yourself you enjoy and never let anyone take them away. If you have to, write a new subroutine. Though I haven't seen Joan in years, I hope she's having a wonderful life. And I hope she still whistles.

GEORDI

Blind Lieutenant Commander Geordi La Forge (LeVar Burton):
a man with clear perspective and a good outlook.

Jeepers, creepers, where'd you get those peepers? This is
supposed to be the height of 24th-century optical technology? The chief engineer wearing a barrette over his
eyes? Come on, you know it's a barrette; I know it's a barrette.

More than the spectacular space battles, the million-dollar sets, and the expensive latex-skinned aliens, Geordi La Forge's VISOR is my favorite *Star Trek* special effect.

I've never liked to wear glasses myself. Not even sunglasses. First, I tend to lose them. Second, I'm kind of vain.

As the years gather momentum, my once-sharp eyes have become very average. This has turned into a mixed blessing. I can't read the newspaper in the dark anymore, but—and this is a big upside—everybody looks better.

I've put a diffusion lens on my life. Cinematographers use diffusion to create soft focus. Soft focus can hide small wrinkles and imperfections on the faces of screen idols. A well-known cameraman was once asked what he shot through to make an aging Bette Davis appear beautiful. A bath towel, he replied.

A great story. It might even be true. But let's get back to La Forge. His eyewear is interesting, but it isn't the basis of his character or life. This is: Geordi has the best sense of humor on *The Next Generation*.

His gift is being able to see the humanity in everyone. The lieutenant commander is quick with a smile and a laugh. He disarms Worf. He's virtually adopted Data, Barclay, and Wesley. Each has become a special friend.

It was Geordi who saw an individual Borg as more than a part of the collective. Geordi who talked and listened to and came to understand an enemy. Geordi who made that enemy a friend. Our barrette-eyed engineer even found and brought out humanity in a machine species.

He even sees the humanity in the warp engines. When they were ailing in the episode "Booby Trap," he created a holodeck version of their mother. Together they nursed the warp drive back to health.

The Next Generation has always been saturated with irony. But here is one of the best. The crew member with a barrette over his eyes sees things most clearly of all.

WORF

Advertising is a service business, and I've met all sorts of clients. Some are easy to like, good people whom I've come to regard as friends. Others…well, it takes all kinds to make a world.

On rare occasions I have to deal with a nasty client, a real stinkaroo. Sad but true. In that situation I have no choice. I screw up all my courage. I look 'em in the eye and I find something to like about 'em.

Not pretend that I like 'em. I find some characteristic, some common belief, some *something* to really like. Hey, everybody's got a good point if you can find it. They say Hitler was nice to his dog. Anyway, it's absolutely necessary to find a part to like. Because if you don't, your client will find out. More importantly, it will show in your work.

I consider this part of my job. My clients, even those with less than stellar personalities—names are being withheld to protect the seriously flawed—deserve my respect. I owe it to them. I also owe it to my coworkers not to irritate the source of our income. And I do it for my personal sense of honor.

When it comes to honor, of course, nobody but nobody compares with my favorite ponytailed Klingon, Worf. "Worf." What kind of a name is that, anyway? Is it his first name or last? Maybe it's a nautical name? Could he have a sister Pier or an Uncle Dock? If it is nautical, maybe his full name is Fisherman's Worf. That could explain how that horseshoe crab got stapled to his forehead.

Whatever the origin of his moniker, this guy could be called Mr. Honor. He spent the middle of *The Next Generation* as a Klingon outcast, the son of a traitor. In reality, his father wasn't a traitor. ("Sins of the Father," "Reunion," and "Redemption, Part I" are the

As a Klingon, Worf knows his life isn't insular;
he lives in a much larger context.

key episodes that explain it.) Worf suffered in silence for the greater good of the Klingon Empire. By living as one without honor, he saved the honor of the entire Klingon civilization. This is the kind of stuff that can give you ulcers. Ultimately Worf cleared his name without injuring the reputation of the empire. Not that the Klingon Empire has such a pristine reputation. Attila the Hun could probably win the Klingon Humanitarian (Klingonitarian?) of the Year Award.

Even though he suffered in silence, I'm not suggesting Worf would make a good adman. Although he put his personal feelings aside for the good of the firm, he never really found anything to like about Duras (the Klingon he gave up honor to protect). In fact, he eventually killed Duras. And any practicing advertising executive will tell you, slicing off a client's head with a *bat'leth* could influence the surviving clients to put the account up for review.

Still, Worf understood and accepted the concept of being humble for the greater good. To me, this is the highest form of honor and a very powerful lesson. The world is not all about you. In it there are things we don't like. It is filled with people who treat us badly. Sometimes these people are our clients; sometimes they're our siblings or spouses.

In any case, we have to realize we exist in a larger context. Hating a client and showing it will harm the coworkers we toil beside. Letting your brother-in-law know your true feelings might feel good while you're shouting, but it can wreak havoc in your family. Far better to find something you like about them and get on with your life. And when you do, you'll be getting on with a life filled with honor.

Sitting in an outdoor cafe in Chicago, I gazed up at a huge twenty-story building. Nothing around it was taller than six or seven stories, so it dominated the small piece of the sky into which it rose.

One side showed a beautifully ornamented face. The other walls were a marked contrast, twenty stories of ugly bare brick. No windows. No adornment. No angels in the architecture. No nothin'.

Even though the edifice was blocks away, I knew what side faced the street: the attractive one. The other three sides were left pretty much unfinished. As if the architect thought no one would notice. *Duh!* The building is sticking up in the air like a sore thumb. It's twenty floors tall. The back is every bit as observable as the front. Everyone can see.

It struck me that people are similar to this lazy architectural style. We put on a public persona that faces the street and believe the rest of our personality and thoughts are invisible.

True, no doubt, of most of us, but not of my favorite Klingon. The thing I really love about Worf is that he makes no attempt to hide who he is. Worf is completely comfortable exposing his entire personality to the outside world. As Flip Wilson used to say, "What you see is what you get, honey."

Worf doesn't need to hide because he's true to himself. No ornamented face is needed. Unless you call that bony ridge on his nose an ornament. I suppose you could. But I think it would look pretty odd on the hood of my car, let alone on my Christmas tree.

Never mind. What counts is that Worf can be honest to the world because he's honest with himself. Most of us find this difficult to do. Little lies and rationalizations integrate seamlessly into our self-perceptions. We feel safer hiding behind masks, believing we only reveal our street sides to public view.

Surprise. People know who you really are. What kind of person you are. You will be judged on your whole as a human being, not just your best face. You are a twenty-story building walking through life. People see all sides of you.

There's a wonderful lesson in this for those of us brave enough to follow. The more honest we are with ourselves, the less time we have to spend constructing a mask. Hey, folks are going to see you for who you are—whether you want them to or not. So we might as well follow the example of our Klingon friend.

I'm not saying this is easy. In fact I believe it is extremely difficult. And maybe it takes a warrior's heart like Worf's to face the world without a facade.

BEVERLY CRUSHER

I got a cold this spring. I get a cold every spring. Same cold, same symptoms, it always lasts about three days, then disappears until it shows up again the following spring.

I get this doctor every spring to treat the cold. Different doctor, different office, he always says the same thing. Take an antihistamine. Gargle with warm salty water. Drink plenty of fluids. Call me if it gets any worse.

What bothers me about this medical advice is that it's identical to the way my mom treated my colds when I was a kid. That was over thirty years ago. What on earth have doctors been doing in the meantime? What about the National Institutes of Health, the Centers for Disease Control, the Ponds Institute? I mean, what are they doing, really?

Let's take a look at your basic cold. A virus invades your body. You get sick. Your body produces antibodies that combat and defeat the virus. You get well.

Some of those antibodies even remain on guard for that specific virus so it can never get you again. Here's the rub. Those antibodies have the intelligence of Clark Kent's coworkers at the *Daily Planet*. When the virus comes back next year, it mutates a little, puts on eyeglasses or a new hat, and the antibodies don't recognize the cleverly disguised virus. *Wham*—you're sick again. Et cetera, et cetera, et cetera.

In our century, medicine has neatly divided itself into two chunks. Mom as *Dr. Quinn, Medicine Woman,* warm and loving, with a host of folk remedies. And the cold, unsatisfying medical technologists who insist on verifying your medical plan before scanning a hangnail in a magnetic resonance imaging machine.

There is one doctor who fulfills both roles, but you won't find her in a hospital. You'll have to check sickbay. It's Doctor Mom, Beverly Crusher.

Beverly is more than competent on both counts, whipping up equal portions of tricorder knowledge and maternal wisdom. She's a bit opinionated and preachy (like McCoy before her). But, for me, her most important feature is that her heart is in the right place. Not insignificant for such a vital organ.

In sickbay, she's cool and in command. Her medical charges function as a well-drilled team. The extras in the background in every episode of *The Next Generation* move very crisply in their blue science uniforms. Yet all this efficiency is balanced by her respect for life. Not only when the patient is in danger, but when she treats

As physician and mother, Dr. Beverly Crusher (Gates McFadden) demonstrates that the most important component of good living is having a heart in the right place.

the people who are not sick, her sickbay staff. She's considerate, understanding, and caring.

At home with Wesley, her son, she shows a mother's love. Once again, she strikes a balance of discipline and freedom. She's raised a bright, intelligent, courteous son. Hell, from a parent's point of view, Wesley is perfect.

Her relationship to Jean-Luc is another example. On a professional level it remains, well, professional. On a personal level, they care about and trust each other. And though there is a greater depth to their emotion, Beverly lets Picard know it's there without ever crossing a line or acting inappropriately.

Her heart isn't only in the right place, it's in perfect rhythm. She's a career woman, a mother, and a good friend, with everything in balance. She has a sense of what she's already achieved and of her potential. She knows how much she has to give. She knows what makes her happy. And that lets her keep her life in balance. It's almost too bad Wesley is a boy. Beverly Crusher would be the perfect mom to follow to the job on "Take Your Daughter to Work Day."

Which is great except next spring my cold will be back. And where will Dr. Crusher be when I need Vicks VapoRub spread on my chest? Right between my toes on my television screen as I watch *The Next Generation* reruns from my bed and wait out the virus.

DEANNA TROI

*T*he universe is unimaginably big, inconceivably large, until you stub your toe.

An earthquake that leaves ten thousand dead in India doesn't have the impact on my life that a stopped-up toilet does. I realized this when I discovered that the newspaper I was using to soak water off my bathroom floor had a story about a terrible earthquake. This odd ranking of priorities made me crazy when I thought about it—which, mercifully, I didn't for very long, as my attention was concentrated on sopping up the mess.

Later my mind drifted back to the subject, and I decided that this wasn't a personal defect; rather, it was one associated with my species. I'm a human, and we humans are incredibly selfish beings. We judge the relative importance of things in concentric circles beginning at our noses.

On second thought, I decided that my first thought was too harsh. Try this on. If we become too empathic, we can't survive. This isn't a fault; it's a defense mechanism. No single person could possibly share all the pain and suffering that's taking place in the world at any given moment without going mad. Heck, I couldn't maintain my sanity if I shared the pain and suffering from the average Kenny G concert.

Deanna Troi does it every day. No, she doesn't listen to Kenny G. From my understanding of *Star Trek* history, Kenny G was killed in the eugenics wars. (This was followed by forty years of peace until a future archaeologist uncovered the buried remains of some John Tesh CDs and the earth plunged into a dark age.)

Counselor Troi feels what those around her feel. She

Deanna Troi shows us that a little empathy goes a long way.

really feels their pain, their joy, their confusion. Sometimes this is a tremendous advantage. She's a living lie detector, helping Captain Picard with critical information on opponents. In many episodes, her ability to sense emotion has saved the ship. Not inconsequentially, it makes her a formidable poker player.

Still, I get the sense that the producers of *The Next Generation* really didn't know what to do with Deanna Troi. They started her out as a key member of the bridge crew. Troi, Riker, and Picard forming the three-legged stool of command. The three chairs on the bridge of the *Enterprise*-D were for them.

Later she drifted as sort of a pleasant diversion. A nice piece of scenery without any real role. She was the ship's therapist and became the surrogate mother of Alexander (Worf's son).

Deanna Troi never relented. She gave every job her full energy and enthusiasm. She stayed fiercely loyal to her captain and crewmates. She maintained her poise and focus. Eventually she worked her way back to the command structure on the bridge. And she did it all while listening to the problems of the world.

She understands that you can be empathic while still maintaining a discreet distance. That's why, rather than solving the problems of the people who come to her, she helps them to solve the problems by themselves.

When Worf had trouble with Alexander, Troi was there. Not to replace Worf, but to help him find the time and opportunities to share his son's life. To encourage him to attend the *Enterprise* equivalent of PTA meetings (not easy for a Klingon). To foster the natural bond of father and son.

She even overcame her own empathic instincts, ordering a crew member on a suicide mission when it became necessary for the survival of the ship—a gut-wrenching personal exploration of the emotional difference between being a counselor and being a commander.

I really think the lesson Deanna reveals to us is how to accept emotion without succumbing to it. To enjoy it for what it is.

Sometimes, we are so self-absorbed that something as minor as a broken toilet can be the number-one priority in our lives. Conversely, we can get so wrapped up in the problems of others that we nearly drown in their emotions. The key is not to get in over your head in either situation because, let's face it, there's never a plumber around when you really need one.

Empathy is a good thing; so is toilet paper. It's important to understand that too much of either can stop up the works.

LWAXANA TROI

She started out as Number One in the original *Star Trek* pilot, "The Cage." Later, after the second pilot gave birth to a series, she portrayed Nurse Chapel. She played Deanna Troi's mother, Lwaxana, on *The Next Generation* and reprised that character on *Deep Space Nine*. If the computers on the four *Star Trek* series and the various *Star Trek* movies sound familiar, it's because she gives voice to them all. She has appeared on screen in almost every *Star Trek* film. In real life, Gene Roddenberry married her. Scientists believe the universe is held together by invisible dark matter. I think it's held together by Majel Barrett.

Let's face it: Without Majel Barrett, *Star Trek* would be impossible.

Of all her roles, the one I like least but have learned the most from is Lwaxana. This Betazoid matron is loud, overbearing, pushy, and rude. A more unlikable amalgam of unfavorable personality traits is unimaginable.

Lwaxana Troi (Majel Barrett) is as keen a judge
of character as they come.

Robbie Robinson

Behind the pomposity, however, is an unerring
instinct. Aw, hell, what it is, is wisdom. She knows
exactly what's wrong or right with people (or Klingons
or Betazoids or Whatevers). Even worse, she knows
that she knows.

With little Alexander, Worf's son, she cuts through the
years between them and gives him a sense of worth. She
understands his rebellion and turns it into positive fun.

With Odo, the nearly inflexible shape-shifter from
Deep Space Nine, Lwaxana penetrates his crusty exte-
rior and finds the warmth and dignity inside.

She's knows exactly how far to push Jean-Luc Picard
to get her way. It's her game, and in it the captain is a
pawn; Lwaxana is the queen.

With her daughter Deanna, she is almost omniscient. Before the counselor knows her own heart, her mother does.

And it goes on and on and on. It took me a while to discover this side of Lwaxana. Blinded by her obnoxious ways, all I could see were her flaws.

Not quite as drastic but every bit as revealing was my real-life introduction to Lee. Lee is an Air Force sergeant. During our first encounter, Lee exhibited military detachment and coolness. When I meet folks of this rank, I expect a barrel-chested, gruff-talkin', cigar-chompin' tough guy.

Instead, Lee was an attractive, athletic female. Still, I attributed some of the less attractive aspects of the military personality to her. I mean, c'mon, what kind of a woman would want to push her way up the chain of command in the Air Force?

I'll tell you what kind of a woman. An intelligent woman with a great sense of humor. Overcoming my prejudice took a little time. But it was well worth it. Lee turned out to be an interesting person. Her military ambition was only part of the whole. It's a lesson that Lwaxana was trying to teach me. I hope I never forget it.

A "LIGHT" DIVERSION

My favorite addition to *The Next Generation* isn't a character. It's the holodeck. I want one. Basically, the holodeck is your Nintendo on steroids. It can conjure up any time or place you choose, even create the people you want to be with. Then you can interact with the creation. Jean-Luc plays detective in there. Worf uses it for calisthenics.

I've got plenty of room for it. It could double as my bedroom. When I'm not transforming it into Fenway Park, the Lunar Excursion Module, or that island Wonder Woman comes from, I'd just turn it into the Presidential suite at the Ritz-Carlton.

Problem is, I'd probably never leave. I suppose I could invite all my friends over. But why bother? Why not just create new and improved versions of my friends? You know, adjust Mike Brown's political views to coincide more closely with mine. Make my sister Amber just a little less domineering. Change an irritating laugh here, or an abrasive impulse there.

No reason to stop there. I could create "Dave's America." Populate it with attractive artists, musicians, and scientists; eliminate disease, poverty, war, Barney. Put a 4,000-foot vertical-drop ski resort right next to the tropical reef with 150 feet of underwater visibility.

Dave's cable system would include the *Star Trek* channel. Pay-per-view would mean the channel pays me every time I turn it on. *It's a Wonderful Life* would play only once during the holiday season. Oh yeah, every day would be Christmas. And most important, *Dave's World* would not be about Dave Barry; it would be about me.

Hence, we've run headlong into the nexus problem. In the movie *Star Trek Generations*, Kirk and Picard are happy as clams, living perfect lives in the nexus: no struggle, no challenge. Just perfect bliss.

Bliss turns out to be boring as heck. (Exactly as I predicted, I might point out, in *All I Really Need to Know I Learned from Watching Star Trek*.) It's not real. Kirk and Picard choose to face danger in the real world rather than experience utopia in a fantasy.

I'm not sure I'd be as strong. The prospect of my own holodeck is intriguing at the very least. I would like to think that I'd come out eventually, maybe in a couple of years. That the touch of humanity with all its imperfections and scars is better because it's real.

I guess my sister Amber wouldn't be the same if she were less assertive, and maybe the basis of my friendship with Mike is the intellectual challenge he provides

Like *Star Trek* fans and their TV sets, Riker and Picard use the holodeck to enjoy a brief escape from the hustle and bustle of their daily routine.

Elliott Marks

with his erroneous political views. What's important is how we survive in a world that doesn't bend to our whims. How we shape our lives and our environment. How we triumph and fail. These could never be achieved in a holodeck.

Of course, I still want one.

WESLEY CRUSHER

L i'l Wesley Crusher. When I was in school we hated kids like Wesley. A great student, Goody Two-Shoes, the captain's pet, mama's boy. Any of these reasons alone would have made him uncool. He's got 'em all, plus a new one that didn't exist when I attended St. Joe's: computer geek.

I know the Wesley character was an attempt to reach out to kids. But he's like no kid I ever met. First of all, why didn't he get acne? The rest of us had to suffer through it. And don't tell me they cured pimples in the 24th century. We need oil and white blood cells to survive. Without the stuff that zits are made of we'd be sickly piles of sand. Like, I'm sure he just wiped his face to healthy perfection with Oxy-googol.

Then there's this idea of a adolescent ensign on the bridge. What's next? Doogie Howser in sickbay? A baby in engineering? Let's get a grip.

Although for the most part Wesley drove me crazy, I believe the actor that played him did a tremendous job.

How could Wesley get so far under my skin if Wil Wheaton didn't portray him so convincingly? Right down to that ingratiating little smile.

And let's not forget that Wesley did save the ship from that asteroid. In fact, he had a lot of high notes during the series. My favorite was an episode called "The Game." Here's where Wesley's unnatural instincts once again save the *Enterprise*.

Ensign Wesley Crusher (Wil Wheaton).

We're talking about a mind-control game that is brought aboard the ship. Anyone who plays it falls under the spell of bad aliens who want to take over the Federation. Everybody plays it, almost. Wesley, an arcade-age teenager, never engages in the game. This is nuts. He should have been the first one to try it. Here he is, right in the middle of his Nintendo years, and he doesn't play. This is all the proof I need that there is something seriously wrong with the lad.

But by not playing, he avoids the spell of the bad aliens and, along with Data, saves the day. Thing is, this is one of my favorite episodes. It's got a nice "Invasion of the Body Snatchers" kinda feel. It's very well done, and you end up rooting for Wesley as the bad guys close in.

Throughout the entire series Wesley lived everybody's life but his own. In engineering, he was Little La Forge. He went to the academy seeking Picard's approval. I always got the feeling Wesley was trying to please somebody.

Finally, and I really do mean finally, Wesley's sense of self showed up. In almost the last episode, Wesley put childish things aside and listened to himself. He left Starfleet Academy. He stopped looking to others to show him the way, and he headed into an uncertain future.

It took seven seasons for the boy to become a man. But he did it. He did it by being true to himself. Or maybe he just grew up.

You know, there are a lot of kids out there like Wesley—computer dweebs, mama's boys, teacher's pets. You may not suspect this but I wasn't the most popular kid in my class. I was sort of a skinny goof.

Thankfully, childhood is a curable disease. It just takes time. The best prescription is to enjoy every second of it having the most fun possible. Don't try to be an adult when you're a kid; it's a losing proposition.

Wesley Crusher tried to grow up too soon, and he seemed lost most of the time. But he did give us one important lesson. Even the most annoying kid has plenty of time to find himself and go on to do something great.

TASHA YAR

*T*asha Yar. Lotsa tar. That's what did her in. Killed by an oil slick, like a mastodon in the La Brea tar pits. Slimed like a ten-year-old on Nickelodeon. Her life washed away by the Jiffy Lube monster. Tasha, we hardly knew ye.

When *The Next Generation* premiered, Security Chief Natasha Yar played a major role. Strong, beautiful, professional: the epitome of a well-scrubbed Starfleet officer. Her uniform also signaled a change from *The Original Series*. Back then, the security officers wore red shirts. These red shirts, rarely worn by regular cast members, became a terrible omen. They foreshadowed certain death before the first commercial. Tasha never wore the red shirt, but she suffered the same fate.

Gene Roddenberry was a Los Angeles policeman before he was a television writer. He saw how men died on the street. Quickly, unexpectedly, very often meaninglessly.

Tasha's death was much the same. Here one minute,

Lieutenant Natasha Yar (Denise Crosby),
living her too-brief life to the fullest.

Robbie Robinson

ready for recycling at your neighborhood Amoco the
next. And then the series moved on.

But if *Star Trek* teaches us one thing, it's that death is
just a stage on the way to resurrection. Spock, Scotty,
Riker, and Lore have died and come back. I'm sure
Kirk will be back faster than you can say "millions."
Personally, when I go, I'd like to be buried on the
Genesis planet like Spock. Soft-land me in a photon
torpedo tube, then come back in a year or two, so I can
get on with my life.

And so too, Tasha came back. First as herself in the
alternate reality of "Yesterday's *Enterprise*," then as
her own daughter in "Redemption, Parts I and II." I
know this sounds like an Appalachian inbreeding

thing, but it was actually a temporal disturbance/ Romulan-human crossbreeding thing.

Confused? Well, who isn't? Now, back to my original point, which, I believe, had to do with Tasha's death in the original timeline....

Although being drowned by the Jiffy Lube monster isn't a very dramatic or dignified way to go, Tasha died doing something she loved. She knew the risks of her work. Like the police officers that protect and serve our communities, she chose to put on the uniform. Because of that choice, her death, while sudden, wasn't meaningless.

When I think of the *Challenger* astronauts, I feel the same way. Space is a dangerous and risky place. The astronauts in that ill-fated shuttle chose to be there. They chose to live part of their lives in space. The consequence of living in space is that people will surely die there. All life ends, even here on earth. But to die doing something you love, that you believe in, that you are dedicated to, that you choose, means you understand how to live.

The lesson of Tasha Yar isn't about death. It's about life. I hope we all choose so well.

GUINAN

*E*arly tribes of humans ascribed their existence to the favor of gods. The moon god ruled the night until chased away by the sun god. When the sun god overstayed his welcome, the people prayed to the rain god. Gradually science deposed these deities. But science will never dispose of man's spiritual nature.

Growing up Catholic, my spiritual nature was nurtured by the nuns at St. Joseph School. Nurtured may be too gentle a word. In those days, the church thought the best way to get us to heaven was to beat the hell out of us.

Come Sundays, my spiritual needs were administered to by the priests of St. Patrick parish, where I was an altar boy. As part of my ritual duties I served wine to the celebrants of the Holy Mass. In retrospect, I've wondered if this act meant I was a bartender as a minor.

Maybe. Maybe not. But I certainly am not the first human to make the connection between spirits and spirituality.

As an adult I've know many a man who searched for spirituality on a barstool. I did a little of it myself. Why not? Right behind the bar are bottles filled with spirits. It makes the search less strenuous.

I suppose, then, it's more than coincidence that the most spiritual character on *The Next Generation* resides under one of the bartenders' flat hats. Guinan, like any good bartender, knows when either your glass or your soul is empty.

One last note on liquor and spirituality. I agree with Kurt Vonnegut. *PLEASE NOTE: THIS IS A WARNING.* If you drink all the liquor and do all the drugs you can possibly ingest, you *will* see God. Darn soon, too!

OK, back to Guinan. She reminds us there's a world beyond the visible. Beyond what we can see, hear, and touch. Her senses go beyond those of the captain and crew of the *Enterprise*-D.

In "Yesterday's *Enterprise*," she isn't even sure what those senses are telling her; she just knows something isn't right. In this episode reality is altered; a temporal rift has stolen the *Enterprise*-C from an earlier time and changed the course of history, putting both *Starships Enterprise* into the middle of a galactic war. Only Guinan perceives the change.

She rejects all the physical evidence of this new history and trusts her intuition, imploring the captain to return the *Enterprise*-C to its own time. More remarkably, Picard trusts her. He goes beyond science.

His belief in Guinan's instincts is an exercise in faith. This faith is what allows the ship to be saved and the war to be avoided. They find peace.

Neither Picard nor Guinan is bound by what they can see, touch, or feel. More important, both are willing to be taken where this openness leads them. Once there, they accept what they find as real.

Personally, I've already made the leap. I accept spiritual forces to be as real as one of Sister Mary Marie's backhanders. To paraphrase a great science-fiction writer, the universe isn't just greater than we comprehend, it's greater than we *can* comprehend.

There is no science to explain love or wonder. But they are as real as the moon, the sun, and the rain. They are greater. They make our lives meaningful. They make our lives worth living.

Science and technology can describe our universe, but they cannot explain what part we play in the universe or why. There are other voices for us to hear. If we are open enough and brave enough to listen and accept.

RO LAREN

About the dumbest thing on our planet is the difference between men's and women's bicycles. Male bikes have a bar that sits devastatingly close to a man's—how shall I say this?—fragile underside.

Female bikes do not have this unnecessary design flaw. Which leads me to believe women invented the bicycle as a sort of practical joke. Even if this is true, I'm not upset with the gals for having a little fun. Let's face it, women usually end up with the short end of the stick.

If you need proof, which you shouldn't, just look at Ensign Ro Laren.

Ro resented Picard and came to admire him. She detested and then found herself attracted to Riker. She infiltrated the Maquis and then joined them. A sexist might say she was just exercising a woman's prerogative to change her mind. But Laren doesn't fit the profile of a confused anyone.

She is a strong, intelligent, independent woman. Exactly the kind of woman I'm drawn to. And there's my problem. If there is one thing a strong, intelligent, independent woman doesn't need, it's me. Never mind.

If Ro Laren's (Michelle Forbes) difficult life teaches anything,
it's the importance of being true to oneself.

Hey, the point is that independent women have hard choices to make. That's true in our century and apparently will continue in the 24th century. But when I look at Ro, her choices are impossible. She's a walking *Kobayashi Maru*. Take a look.

In the penultimate episode of *The Next Generation*, she finds a cause she believes in: the Maquis. Of course she only finds it because she is ordered to infiltrate it as a spy. To follow her conscience and be true to the Maquis, she must betray Jean-Luc Picard, who had become her friend and ally.

So here's her choice: stay true to her friend or true to her own beliefs. No middle ground.

If that's not bad enough, her Maquis mentor—a man much like her own father—a kind, caring, gentle friend, is killed before her eyes.

I mean, *wow!* I know some *Star Trek* characters have faced serious trauma, but this is bordering on abuse. What's next? Canceling her subscription to *Guns & Ammo*?

Still she survives. She perseveres. No matter how horribly she is treated in the series, Ro toughs it out, learns a little, and moves on. If adversity builds strength, then Ro is made of depleted uranium.

When I watch her, she's a reminder of how tough life can be for strong, independent women. I'm closer to this than you might think. I've three sisters, all of whom are navigating successful careers. Without a doubt, genetics played a part—my mom was an oak. I see Ro in all of them.

I know this is something I'll never truly understand from my side of the gender divide. But I sure do admire it.

HUGH

*O*ne very unusual featured character on *The Next Generation* came from a society based on complete conformity. Using him to explore individuality is the type of concept that reveals the best of *Star Trek*. But don't let me drone on.

Hugh is a Borg. The Borg are a part-biological, part-machine society. In Borg circles they call themselves "the collective." (I believe this is a slightly veiled reference to communism.) They've taken Pink Floyd's "all in all you're just another brick in the wall" philosophy to an absurd extreme. Everyone thinks, feels, and does the same things.

They dress uniformly like Roto Rooter men in rubber wet suits. Tubes run in and out of everywhere. They walk with a funny side-to-side motion that makes them look like they have to go to the bathroom. I assume, however, they don't ever go the bathroom, because by the time a person got out of that suit it would be too late. Besides, with their collective consciousness, when one of them has to go, they all have to go. Geez, no wonder they're so ornery.

Most Borg only speak a smidgen of English. Apparently the only phrases in the Borg-to-English Dictionary are "You will be assimilated" and "Resistance is futile." There is no Borg literature, dance, or art. In short, hanging out with the Borg is like living in Terre Haute, Indiana.

Despite a lifetime of forced conformity, Hugh (Jonathan Del Arco) learned to express himself as an individual.

Danny Feld

Introduced in the episode, "I, Borg," Hugh was the sole survivor of a Borg spaceship crash. Subsequently the *Enterprise*-D stumbled upon him, and he became a prisoner of the Federation. At the time his name wasn't Hugh. Third of Five was his Borg designation. Among the Borg this is a popular name like Smith or Johnson.

Aboard the *Enterprise*-D, Geordi named him Hugh

after they started to become friends. More than Hugh's name changed during his stay on the ship. Slowly, Hugh and the crew (nice rhyme) learned about each other. Two completely different cultures found common ground.

This is not to say the relationship was satisfactory to everyone. Picard had Geordi design an invasive program like a computer virus for Hugh. This virus would do more than give Hugh the flu. Carried back to the Borg collective, the virus had the potential to put the Borg on the endangered species list. Consequently—especially to Hugh—Hugh would die in the epidemic.

Time and understanding defeated these vengeful impulses. Hugh was returned safely to the Borg, with a weapon perhaps more powerful than the virus: a sense of self, an identity as an individual.

Working for an older, wiser creative director in an advertising agency, I had a similar experience. I was interviewing for a position at the time. My previous agency had been a place of little discipline, at least for me. The shop with which I contemplated taking employment was considered to be much more conservative. Wondering how I would make the adjustment, the creative director asked if I could fit in at the new surroundings. "I can adjust to any system." I replied.

The CD looked at me and said, "I've always felt I can make any system adjust to me." This was a revelation to the young adman who was sitting in my seat. It changed the way I looked at my career and myself.

Like Hugh, I was given the chance to be myself, to express my individuality. I came to realize that my particular way of viewing the world had value. From that point on I've striven to bring the things that make me an individual to any system in which I worked. Yeah, I've made adjustments to fit in. But I never gave up the things that make me unique, that make me—*me*. I also believe that the system adjusted to me, and my contributions made us both better.

The lesson of Hugh is powerful. Even the most rigid system, one that demands total conformity, cannot exist without the individuals that make it up. Without individuals, without individuality, there's nothing. Only through expressing yourself can you make a difference. Hugh learned it on the *Enterprise*. I learned it in a corner office at Foote, Cone & Belding. And we're both better because of it.

Q

I will never be confused with Bob Vila. Good news for Bob, no doubt. Still, occasionally I lift a hammer or turn a screwdriver. One such incident occurred recently.

The door on my back deck began to sag. This made it difficult to open or close. As opening and closing are the main functions of a door, this proved an inconvenience. So it came to be that I found myself with a screwdriver, impersonating Barney.

No. I am not referring to the singing purple dinosaur. How could that thing even hold a screwdriver? I mean, those stubby little forearms are not the appendages of a tool user. Of course a dinosaur could just smash through the deck, alleviating the need for a door altogether. No. The Barney I'm talking about is the one from *Mission: Impossible*.

Oh yeah, one more thing about the crooning purple *T. rex*. That "I love you" song is a stolen tune. The real words are "Knick-knack-patty-whack give the dog a bone, this old man came rolling home." I know it. You know it. Our silence is a part of this terrible crime. Let's stop him now before he starts stealing cars.

Barney from *Mission: Impossible* could do anything with a screwdriver. By the way, Barney was on the original *Mission: Impossible*, the one where Leonard Nimoy played Paris, not the new *Mission: Impossible* that came later, and certainly not the movie *Mission: Impossible*, which starred Tom Cruise. If you ever feel the need to watch the original *Mission: Impossible*, it seems to run on FX virtually 24 hours a day. Anyhow, Barney could do anything with a screwdriver. Uplink a satellite? No problem. Bust a political prisoner out of jail? Just twist slowly and carefully. Amazing guy, this Barney.

Unfortunately, neither Barney was on the deck with me. So there I was holding a screwdriver. As I started to work on the top hinge, a rusty screw refused to cooperate. I applied pressure and pushed in with all my strength until finally the screw started to come out.

Odd thing about that. To extract a screw, push in hard. Exactly the opposite of what seems right. Pushing in helps it come out. Counterintuitive.

And that brings me to Jean-Luc Picard's personal devil, Q. Q is the absolute opposite of the flying Frenchman. In fact, most of his behavior seems intentionally annoying. As Data noted in "All Good Things...," Q treats Picard like a favored pet. Playing with him. Teasing him. Testing him to see his abilities. Picard, of course, refuses to play along. As a pet, the captain is more cat than dog.

I disagree with Data. I think Q is Jean-Luc's best

friend. Stay with me. Q is just the opposite of what we think a friend should be. Obnoxious, self-centered, and mean-spirited. Of course, that's the exact behavior exhibited by humans who believe they are omnipotent. In Q's case, however, we should grant him a little latitude. He *is* omnipotent.

The example of Q (John DeLancie) teaches us to look beneath the surface to find real meaning.

Robbie Robinson

The thing is, as terribly as he acts, he's a good guy. The more petty his behavior, the more likely he's preventing some enormous disaster. And with each new encounter, the captain and crew of the *Enterprise*-D learn more about the universe and themselves. At his absolute sadistic worst in "All Good Things...," he guides Picard to saving the entire human species. What more could you ask of a best friend?

Nothing about Q is as it should be. That is to say, Q doesn't conform to our expectations. Why should he? He is a godlike being. Let him set his own standards.

Q is like that friend who will embarrass you in a group but always comes through in the clutch. And in the end, that's OK. We shouldn't demand our friends fit our ideas of how they should act. Not if we want to keep them as friends.

Hey, the world doesn't always act the way we think it should. Sometimes it's counterintuitive. We should learn from that. Occasionally, a change in perspective can help us see more clearly. Sometimes to get a screw out, push in hard.

FURTHER EXPLORATIONS

An ounce of appearance is worth a pound of performance.

It's a terrible thing but it's true. It's why grown-ups are fooled by that polite, well-dressed little kid with larceny in his heart. I know, I've been a victim. It happened in that exotic locale known as St. Joseph Grammar School in Enfield, Connecticut.

I had finished my lunch and was returning my empty milk carton to the case near Sister Mary Marie's desk. I knew the drill. I was a pro. Each carton was to be neatly put on the lowest row available and adjacent to the other cartons that had already been returned. Each carton should stand straight. No sideways. No tilting. And for God's sake, never ever upside down.

John and I arrived at the front of the room simultaneously. I set my carton down. Nice. Neat. Correctly.

John, in setting down his carton, bumped mine. A small bump, but it might as well have been the collision of the subcontinent of India crashing into Asia and producing the Himalayas for the effect it was about to have on my small world.

As I turned to walk back to my desk a bellow exploded from the front of the room. "Mr. Marinaccio, is this your milk carton?" In reality it wasn't. It was John's. But when the voice of God is booming, the last word you should utter is "No." I did the only thing I could. I stood silently.

John stood silently beside me. As the waves of sound roared over us, we provided a stark contrast. John was tall and had good posture and a neat appearance—the consummate fourth grader. I was skinny, with my shirt-tail hanging out. "Generally disheveled" would have been an apt description.

I don't blame Sister Mary Marie for automatically assuming my guilt. One look would have convinced anyone I was obviously responsible for the mess in the milk case. And in the strange world of Catholic grade school, the only one who could declare my innocence was John. Speaking in my own defense would only buy me more trouble.

Appearances had become reality. This is a truly important concept. It explains Catholic schools, presidential elections, why policemen wear uniforms, the high price of a Wolfgang Puck frozen pizza, and a lot more.

The crew of the *Enterprise*-D uses the power of appearance in "The Emissary." About to stir a sleeping Klingon ship out of an eighty-year nap, Picard lets Worf play the role of captain. As the Klingons awake and see the Federation starship, they prepare for battle—until they see the captain is one of their own. The Klingons stand down. An ounce of appearance avoids a battle.

In the ensuing years, I've cleaned up my act considerably. I'm still not as good a fourth-grader as John…but hey, in business situations I dress the part, and when necessary I've even put gel in my hair.

I'm not saying that appearance can totally replace performance. At some point you better have the goods. But beware. Sometimes you're going to be judged on what you appear to be. It's sad. It's also true.

When I was a kid, a common refrain around the dinner table was "Finish your plate. There are children starving in China." Now, decades later I read that over 50% of Americans are overweight. Hummm, I wonder?

Actually I don't wonder. The most common results of human actions are unintended side effects. More often than not these unexpected consequences turn out to be the most important effects of all.

Take the interstate highway system. Designed to bring the country together, it fueled the flight to the suburbs and the decline of the inner city, and segregated the races. Not exactly what Eisenhower planned.

The Next Generation has illustrated this on numerous occasions, never more superbly than during a visit to the Darwin Station in "Unnatural Selection." The colony was a research outpost dedicated to the advancement of the human species. Its scientists genetically altered their own offspring. Their intention was to produce a better human.

Telepathic children that were physically and mentally superior to the parents were created. Aggressive immune systems protected the progeny from all disease. A wonderful achievement, except...

Except the immune system produced antibodies so powerful they not only prevented infections, they sought out and destroyed viruses at the source. In the bodies of anyone who came in contact with them.

Say you went to a party thrown by these kids. Say you had a cold. Antibodies from the children would attack you and destroy the cold at the source. Ergo the kids could party all night without worrying. You, however, would die. This would not allow you to have any fun at the party.

On the show, these aggressive antibodies completely wiped out the crew of a starship. By the end of the episode, Darwin Station was quarantined indefinitely.

The pursuit of producing perfect humans produced perfect antibodies. And the humans ended up in eternal isolation. A completely unintended effect.

All of this isn't some fancy way of blaming my mother for making me clean my dinner plate, although my battle with the bathroom scale was probably initiated at those childhood suppers.

It is a clear warning about human fallibility. A lesson from my favorite television show. Every action produces a reaction, but it's usually not a reaction we poor, dull humans can predict.

I have a problem with my car. It's paid off.

There are dents in the doors, it requires frequent trips to the mechanic, and the back right tire has a slow leak. Many times I've thought about trading it in, getting something new. But every time I do, one thing holds me back. It's paid off.

No loan payments. Low insurance rates. No reason to get uptight if I bump a concrete pole in a parking lot. Heck, new scratches fit right in.

I understand this is heresy. America is about cars. They say who you are, or who you're not. You are what you drive. Which makes me a ten-year-old Italian ragtop.

One of my favorite things about *Star Trek* is the total absence of cars. Perhaps Gene Roddenberry's greatest joke is basing Starfleet in California and completely eliminating automobiles. Just imagine the Golden State without freeways.

However, it begs the question, what would the crew members drive? Picard probably purchases a Peugeot. Riker is a muscle-car guy, a Corvette. Troi belongs in a Lexus. Geordi would look natural behind the wheel of a pickup truck. Of course, Geordi is blind, so he might have a little trouble getting a driver's license. Then again, his vision isn't much worse than that of some of the other motorists I've encountered. Worf is definitely a four-wheeling Jeep man. Crusher is a doctor, so put her in a Mercedes or BMW. Data is already a clean machine, so let's just stick wheels on him and watch him go.

Better yet, forget what they would drive. It's a fun but meaningless exercise. The measure of the *Enterprise*-D crew is its character. And that's really the point. When Roddenberry got rid of cars, he erased a very silly way to judge a person.

The car you drive, the house you live in—these are window dressing. Anyone who wants to judge me by my beat-up old Alfa is welcome to, but they're completely missing the person inside.

Does it seem that waitresses always wait until your mouth is full to ask you how your dinner is? I mean, they must see you chewing. Do they do it on purpose?

Ever notice this never happens on *Star Trek?* Yes, I know many of our common day-to-day 20th-century experiences never happen on *Star Trek.* That's because there are no restaurants on the *Enterprise.* Sure, there's a bar on the *Enterprise*-D, and that bar does serve some food, but Ten-Forward is more like a VFW hall than a restaurant.

Besides, what I'm driving at isn't really about restaurants. We don't have a restaurant where I work, but we have a kitchen. At lunchtime that kitchen becomes a cross between a high school cafeteria and an episode of *Oprah.* Eating is a social experience.

Don't you think that a common eating area would be well received on the *Enterprise*-D? The first *Enterprise* had one. Just think how maladjusted you'd be if you were to consume every meal alone in your bedroom. C'mon, dirty sheets and socks are great, but they're hardly desired dinner company.

Of course, who knows what illusions would be destroyed if we saw Picard talking with his mouth full? What if Beverly Crusher ate like a pig? And I could happily forgo watching Worf chow down and feel I hadn't missed a thing. Still, the dining room is noticeable by its absence.

Deep Space 9 is like a mall; it has lots of eating places. Even *Voyager* has a mess hall. That furry little Neelix serves as ship's cook and whips up culinary catastrophes in what was formerly the captain's mess. I can't imagine Picard ever agreeing to such a setup.

At my parents' house the dinner table served as sort of a coliseum where nightly battles were watched and engaged in by all. Wherever the dinner table is located, it usually serves as a fulcrum for family life. Often, it's the only place where an entire family will be together during the course of a week.

Without a doubt, if there is space travel on starship scale in the future, I'm sure they'll include a mess hall. I wish the designer of the *Enterprise*-D had included one. I would have liked to see the crew of the *Enterprise*-D sit down for a meal and then have Picard yell "Food fight!"

During my first visit to the Pentagon after joining the National Guard account, I was surprised by what I found in the center of the edifice. After all, this was the bull's-eye for millions of megatons of Soviet nuclear weapons—ground zero. And there in the middle of the courtyard, at the very heart of America's military industrial complex, sat a hot-dog stand. Talk about your red hots.

I could just imagine the scene at the Kremlin. "Igor, aim your warheads at the relish. Ivan, your target is the mustard jar. Comrades, new intelligence reports the buns are stale. We'll need more warheads to get through them."

As I walked through the halls of the Pentagon, some strange feelings percolated. Everyone I met was extremely nice. Courteous. Polite. Helpful. If you're some country considering going to war with America, you couldn't pick nicer folks to be annihiliated by. Really.

Another odd thought crossed my mind. This is Starfleet Command, the 20th-century equivalent anyway. The admirals and captains who were walking the halls had the same demeanor as the hundreds of extras we've seen moving behind Picard or Admiral Cartwright. Which begs the question...

Starfleet is a peaceful organization that values noninterference and scientific exploration above all else, so why is it military-based? There's no doubt it's modeled on the U.S. military in general and the U.S. Navy in particular. Right down to the well-trained bridge crews. Minus Tailhook, of course.

Let's face it, the *Enterprise* has phasers, photon torpedoes, and who knows what other weapons beginning with "ph." Maybe Christopher Lloyd had it right in *Star Trek III: The Search for Spock:* the Genesis Device was intended to wipe out the enemies of the Federation. These guys are loaded for bear.

Nahhh. I don't buy it. *Intent* is what's important here. The Federation wants peace. They act peaceably when given a choice. Even when pushed, Picard is slow to boil. Violence is his last resort.

The bridge of the *Enterprise*-E.

Elliott Marks

What all that firepower comes down to is being prepared. Starfleet likes to be prepared, just like the Boy Scouts. And in a hostile galaxy, that makes pretty good sense.

So arming a ship of peace isn't a contradiction, it's prudent. Like putting a hot-dog stand in the middle of the Pentagon. After all, that very secure building is tough to get into and out of. If you want to have lunch outdoors, the park in the center of the building lets you avoid the guards, X-ray machines, and hassles of actually exiting the place. For convenience there's no better place to have a little lunch stand.

As usual a little thought is better than a first impression. What seems crazy is often sane. Not only that, the little stand serves a decent dog.

I once had dinner with the President of the United States. Just me, George Bush, and four thousand of his closest friends.

A company I worked for had bought seats to a fundraiser. Actually, they bought a whole table. Headquarters was located in New York, so to save a little money they filled out the table with bodies from the Washington field office where I worked. As I had a body, they invited me.

Everyone dressed in tuxedos. Even Barbara Bush wore one. (Just kidding.)

I don't own a tux. Been in one a few times. I'm not exactly James Bond material, but I have to admit I feel kind of cool in a cummerbund and black tie, even if they are rented.

Apparently this is where I part company with Picard and crew. No one on *Star Trek* seems to enjoy getting dressed up. Picard hates formal affairs. The captain turns into a whiner when he has to put on his dress uniform. McCoy, Geordi, whoever—think of a man on *Star Trek,* and he hates formal wear. And please, don't even suggest that Worf put on as much as a blue Burberry blazer.

Now me, some of the best times of my life have happened while I was dressed to the nines. Being part of the wedding parties at the nuptials of my brothers and sisters was a blast. I've picked up a professional award or two while all dressed up. A tux never slowed me down. I've sung, danced, drank, met great-looking women, even gotten stupid.

Dressing to the nines for the best of times: Keiko Ishikawa (Rosalind Chao) at her wedding to Miles O'Brien (Colm Meaney).

I've never understood this tuxedophobia that exists on *Star Trek*. Perhaps a deadly alien species resembles the penguin. Maybe starch started a runaway epidemic. Maybe it's just a lame excuse for some writer to force humor into the script.

Even if the characters don't like to go formal, the actors that play them don't share the phobia. Think about it: All the thespians seem quite comfortable in tuxes when it's award time. Just check out the Oscars or Emmys. For myself, I've enjoyed the few occasions when I've donned formal wear. And I had a heck of a good time in my tux at dinner with the Prez.

Washington, D.C., is a beautiful, culturally rich city. But of all the monuments, museums, parks, and restaurants, the place I like the most is my front stoop.

It's slightly elevated from the street and affords a commanding view all the way to the corner. I've learned a little sitting on the stoop.

Mostly I've observed that people cannot parallel park. They like to try. No sooner does a space become available than the suitors line up. Sometimes they succeed. A lot fail. If you've ever watched a size six woman try to squeeze into a size four dress, you know what I mean. I've witnessed bumps, dents, sideswipes, etc. Apparently the prevailing philosophy of parallel parking is, don't stop until you hear the sound of breaking glass. *Cccrruuuunnchhh!*

Stoop sitting may be going out of style. A few others join me watching the daily parade of Dupont Circle life. My immediate neighbors sometimes take an adjacent seat. Stacy from across the street used to smoke cigarettes on her stoop before she moved. I speculate she did this as a concession to her husband to not smoke in the house. Motorcycle Girl up the corner employs her front porch as a summer dining room. That's about it. A string of empty porches lining both sides of the avenue stretches south for blocks.

For me the stoop is a wonder. It's my window on the world. Or to draw an analogy to my favorite show, it's the viewscreen.

Unlike the *Enterprise,* my porch doesn't travel through the universe, but that's not important. Like the Cytherians, I can explore from my homeworld. In the episode "The Nth Degree," this superintelligent race uses a probe to bring alien species to them. They are, in fact, exactly the same and exactly the opposite of the crew of the *Enterprise*-D. They are explorers whose methods couldn't be more different. They don't seek out strange new life-forms, they sit on the stoop and have the life-forms brought to them.

I hope I share characteristics in common with both species. I like to think I possess the adventurous spirit and drive of the Federation. But it's also nice to sit on the stoop like a Cytherian.

Hey, when you live in the middle of a city, the world will eventually come to your door. I've seen all manner of humanity from the homeless to heads of state. I've watched motorcades, Rollerblades, foreign maids, walkers, and bassinets without moving a muscle. And I've discovered a great truth. On the front porch the world doesn't pass you by; it comes to you.

I read (which really means I saw on a TV show about the English language) that if a person speaks a fourteen-word sentence, then chances are that sentence was never uttered before in the history of mankind. Which means the 37-word sentence you just read is completely uncharted territory. In effect, where no one has gone before. Kinda fun, huh?

Once I learned this fact, I became a much more long-winded speaker. I'm sure most of you will explore some uncharted sentences in the near future as well.

Hey, as a species we're fascinated by unexplored territory. Fairly recently I watched the city of Baltimore go mental because one of their baseball players went where no major-leaguer had gone before. He broke the consecutive-games-played record. I mean, they went absolutely berserk. They held celebrations. Stopped the games. Shot fireworks. All this for consecutive games played. You know, perfect attendance. It wasn't even like the guy got straight A's; he just showed up every day.

But it was a new record, sure to make the Guinness book alongside the longest submarine sandwich and largest ball of tinfoil, so everybody went nuts.

Which, if you think about it, can make our species seem rather silly. I mean, all this hullabaloo over nothing.

Conversely, I believe this trait is also part of humanity's greatest attribute. For while it makes us celebrate meaningless accomplishments, it also makes us strive to explore. To learn something no one else has ever known. To discover what's around the next corner.

I think that's why *Star Trek: The Next Generation* strikes something primal inside of me. Every time I turn on the set, Jean-Luc is pushing to solve a new mystery, probing an unknown gaseous anomaly, looking for an answer. If he's not directly challenging God, he is proving to be the equal of the omnipotent Q.

Even better, everyone on the ship gets to go. The guy who stands in the transporter room. The guy who cleans the bathrooms on Deck 7. The guy who changes the lightbulbs. They all get to go where no one has gone before. And at home on my couch, I get to come along too.

From that same couch I've gotten to share all the great events of our time. We were all there when the Berlin Wall fell, just as our grandfathers shared Lindbergh's flight across the Atlantic.

I may not get to travel around the galaxy or see an extraterrestrial, except on *Star Trek*. But I'll keep watching. My imagination will go. And I'll keep saying and writing fourteen-word sentences that take me where no one has gone before.

George Raft was a famous movie gangster, a contemporary of Cagney and Bogart. Although he was rich and famous, he eventually went bankrupt. He was once asked, "George, you made millions, what happened to your money?" "I spent most of it on wine, women, and song," Raft is reported to have replied. "And the rest I squandered foolishly."

George raises an interesting issue. Is pleasure the most important experience in existence? America's founding fathers thought it was significant; they considered the pursuit of happiness an inalienable right. As with most philosophical questions, this one has been wrestled with on *The Next Generation*.

Of all the planets the *Enterprise* has visited, Rubicun III seems to have been the most hedonistic. The inhabitants, the Edo, were oversexed and underdressed. Little or no interest seemed to be taken in industry or commerce. The entire society was based on the pleasure principle. Needless to say, Riker loved the place.

As friendly as the Edo were, they were also mentally deficient morons. So simple was the society that only one penalty existed for any crime from littering to murder: *Death.* So much for pleasure.

Risa is another planet with similar inclinations. It is, in fact, a galactic *Love Connection,* or if you prefer, a Club Med on a planetary scale. Even Picard got a girlfriend when he went there.

Once again, the inhabitants and visitors pursue pleasure to the exclusion of almost everything else. One of the greatest archaeological treasures in the universe lay buried beneath its surface, and no one was interested enough to pick up a shovel.

On the uptick, the pursuit of pleasure seems a peaceful enterprise. I mean, who wants to fight when you're feeling good? However, hedonism to the exclusion of all else is ultimately shallow.

There's an old conundrum, "Would you rather be a happy pig or an unhappy Socrates?" Picard and the crew of the *Enterprise*-D have given us their answer. While Risa is a nice place to visit, they don't want to live there. Neither would I. Hedonism is great. But I get as much pleasure from learning something new, accomplishing something difficult, or even sometimes trying hard and failing.

Dollars. Pounds. Marks. Francs. Yen. Lire. Pesos. Rubles. Money makes the world go round. Luckily it doesn't make the universe go round. At least, not the universe of *Star Trek*.

Captain Kirk never measures a man, or alien, by the size of his bank account. How could he? I don't believe he ever saw a bank. We certainly never saw him see a bank. We never even knew when it was Kirk's payday.

At the advertising agency where I work it's impossible to miss payday. It's the day everyone is sighing. There is a noticeable increase in activity. People who normally brown-bag it go out to lunch. Coworkers are moaning, "I need a raise," or, "This is already spent." I don't recall these phrases ever being muttered on the *Enterprise*-D. Heck, does anyone even know the name of the currency of the 24th century?

Not that it matters. There's no place to spend money on the *The Next Generation*. The *Enterprise*-D has a bar, Ten-Forward. But no one ever seems to pay at Whoopi's tavern. Of course, the greedy little troll on *Deep Space Nine* has a way of accounting, but let's limit our conversation to humans.

On *The Original Series,* Scotty bought a couple of

drinks on a planet during shore leave once. He ended up on trial for murder.

Uhura tried to buy a tribble on a space station—before she was given the fuzzy little animal as a free sample. And look at the trouble *that* caused.

Hey, could the lesson be that money is the root of all evil? That nothing good ever comes from moolah? One could certainly suppose that's the underlying theme in these shows.

Which is fine except that I don't believe it. Money is money. It's neither good nor evil. Good and evil are found in the same place, the hearts of men and women. Cash is a tool like a hammer or car. Because money is a powerful tool, it tends to magnify good or evil.

In fact, the second most popular phrase in all of *Star Trek* refers, if you stretch your imagination, to wealth. You know, when Spock splits his fingers in the middle: "Live long and prosper." If you don't believe this is a reference to money, think of the antithesis: "Die soon in poverty."

In *Star Trek IV: The Voyage Home,* Kirk told his dinner companion that money wasn't used in the 23rd century. Still, the captain and crew must have been paid something. But what?

Ultimately, I don't think *Star Trek* is making any real point about personal wealth. On the *Enterprise,* a person's worth is judged in a very different way. One's value is measured by what one can contribute to the ship. The most important currency is trust. And when trust, competence, and loyalty are the main characters, money just doesn't play a central role.

A SIDE TRIP TO THE ORIGINAL SERIES

Dr. Leonard McCoy, Captain James T. Kirk, and Commander Spock (DeForest Kelley, William Shatner, and Leonard Nimoy) as they appeared in the original *Star Trek*.

Courtesy the Gregory Jein Collection

The most basic message of *Star Trek* is to get past your prejudices. And I try. But there is a class of people I don't like and never will. They are perhaps the most imperfect humans to inhabit the planet.

Ironically they are known as "perfectionists."

Perfectionists are basically people who don't like your messes. Their own messes are usually OK (to them). In short, they embrace a "do as I say, not as I do" philosophy.

They compare well to another group that prefers others to act in a manner from which it is exempt, the United States Congress. Until recently, each bill passed by Congress contained a little clause which said that the legislative body does not have to obey the law it just enacted. You do, of course. Which leads me to believe Mark Twain was especially accurate when he said, "America has produced no native criminal class except Congress." Clemens uttered that phrase over 100 years ago. Sadly, it still applies.

Back to the point. As to *Star Trek* and perfectionists, one episode did revolve around such a being. A cute little robot called *Nomad*. *Nomad* wasn't always in search of perfection. Early in its childhood *Nomad* was programmed to visit new planets and seek out new life, kind of like a robot *Enterprise*. While on its mission—*blam*—it gets whacked by a meteor.

While the injured tin can is floating in space, it meets *Tan Ru*. *Tan Ru* is an alien probe programmed to retrieve and sterilize soil samples. Together they fuse to become more than the sum of their parts. Unfortunately, they also merge programming and come up with the following twist. Their new, combined mission is to seek out perfect life-forms and to sterilize the imperfect ones. Of course, in the new *Nomad*'s definition, it itself is perfect: it's other people's messes that it can't stand.

Nomad is unequivocally the best example of a perfectionist ever portrayed. It (He? She?) demands absolute perfection from those around it, while being totally blind to its own flaws.

Among other things, *Nomad* is space-happy. It was created by an inventor named Jackson Roykirk. In its new incarnation, it believes James Kirk is its creator. So it doesn't sterilize the imperfect biological infestation (humans) on the *Enterprise*. It listens to the man it mistakes for its creator and obeys his commands. Just like a real perfectionist, *Nomad* just seems to get everything wrong.

I considered this to be one of *Star Trek*'s best episodes. In fact, watch *Star Trek: The Motion Picture* for some amazing similarities. Obviously the producers also thought this was a strong episode.

Star Trek has never been concerned with perfection. The episodes themselves are filled with errors. The concept of warp drive ignores relativity. Speaking of warp drive, sometimes it's incredibly dangerous to go to warp while still in a solar system. On other occasions it is perfectly safe to go into warp just outside of Earth orbit. The *Enterprise* exceeded warp 13 on *The Original Series,* but later warp 10 became the "warp barrier." There are enough examples like this to write a book. In fact, someone did. If the writers and producers of the series had to go back and correct every mistake, they wouldn't have time for any new episodes.

But here's the point. *Star Trek* is about grand theories, not minutiae. *Star Trek* is a great show because it understands that ideas, philosophy, and drama are far more important than making sure all the stardates line up.

Perfectionists focus on the small. Thinkers and achievers focus on the big picture. You know, it's impossible to find a basketball with a microscope. You might find some orange molecules, but you will certainly miss the game. And if you don't watch the game you can't know the score.

Worst of all, they miss the most important point. There is no perfection in life. Nothing and no one is perfect. *Nothing. No One.* PERIOD.

My guess is that humans are probably the least perfect things on the entire galaxy. We're a mess. Most well-adjusted people learn to accept our contradictions and foibles. Want a perfect world? Get rid of the people. Otherwise do what the rest of us have done: join the human race.

WE NOW RETURN YOU TO THE 24TH CENTURY...

The *Enterprise*-D is interesting as much for what's missing as for what's on board. When we look at the gleaming world of the starship, many of the common items of 20th-century life never appear. There are no ashtrays, no sunglasses, and, ironically, no television sets. The conduct of business is also different. What is particularly striking is the way business *isn't* conducted, specifically with paper. The *Starship Enterprise* is the first functioning paperless office I have ever witnessed.

I haven't detected a scrap on board. No computer printouts, no interdepartmental memos, no candy wrappers. Hell, there's not even a roll of Charmin.

Now I've heard about the coming of the paperless office my entire adult life. When computers first appeared, they were supposed to do away with the need for reams of paper. Guess what? They ended up producing more paper than before. Hard copies. That's what the paper that comes out of a computer is called. I don't know why. The computer paper isn't any harder than any other sheet of paper.

The main characteristic of computer hard copies is their ability to disappear at the exact moment you need them. Much like the ability of the computer files to disappear just when you need them. Anyhow, the net result is that there are now just as many files and pieces of paper as there were before, except there's less room to store them because every desk also has a computer on top.

This whole paperwork thing is a little out of whack. Most paperwork is just redoing the real work over again, like memos and conference reports. CYA—cover your rear end—that's what most paper is used for.

Back when I worked for the State of Illinois Department of Mental Health, paperwork was done in place of real work. Each of the mentally retarded adults I supervised had individual developmental programs. Some had tooth-brushing programs, others had arts and crafts programs, and so on. Everyone had a chart where all the programs were recorded. The technicians who ran the programs would then do the paperwork.

The problem was that the technicians discovered it was easier to do the paperwork than to actually run the programs. So instead of spending time teaching a resident to brush his teeth, the tech would just get the resident's chart, fill in the appropriate box, and never get near a toothbrush.

Paperwork replaced real work. Amazingly, most of the supervisors felt this method was just fine. As long as the charts were filled out, everybody was happy.

Well, not everybody. The residents who were being largely ignored weren't so happy.

Some of us didn't go along. We kept real charts. Brushed real teeth. And we got something real out of it: real satisfaction.

Maybe the paperless office exists in the 24th century, but today shuffling parchment is inescapable. Some of it is even necessary. Just never confuse it with real work.

I don't wear a watch. This is not a large liability, except to the Timex Corporation. Somebody usually knows what time it is. And when I'm not sure of the hour, I try to arrive at appointments ahead of time. Ironically, my lack of a wristwatch has made me a very punctual person.

I'm not anti-watch. I've tried to wear one. My problem is a simple one. I lose them. Everything's usually fine for the first few days. Then I take off the watch and forget to put it back on. Then I forget where I took it off. For the next few days I waste more time looking for the damn thing than it could have ever possibly saved me. Finally, frustrated, I give up and I'm out the purchase price of the timepiece.

I have honestly given this a fair shot. I have owned

and lost over a half a dozen watches in my life. I will never lose another.

Besides, no one on *Star Trek* ever wears a wristwatch, either. Not Picard, not Sisko, not Janeway, not Kirk. I actually find that a little odd. You'd think a ship's captain would need to "synchronize his watch" for a special mission. Or in Kirk's case, be on time for a date.

I've never noticed a clock on any *Enterprise*. The only chronometer on the ship is on the navigator's console. About the only time it's ever shown is when it's running backward when the ship travels to the past. Really. We see the digital countdown and the astonished look on the navigator's face. I mean c'mon, time travel is great, but how does the crew know when it's shift change? Is this any way to run a Starfleet?

I've been around military people. The 20th-century kind. They're obsessed with time. Hey, they even have their own special time. Regular old quarter-past-one isn't good enough for these guys. It's always 13:15, 19:30, or 24:00 hours.

I often think the most sophisticated military hardware of our time is the instrument strapped to the wrists of our soldiers. These watches have multiple faces with dials for altitude, barometric pressure, lap times, compasses, and the days of the week. Heck, unless you know precisely where to look, you can't find the time of day.

Star Trek's answer to the immortal question posed by Chicago (the band, not the city), "Does anybody really know what time it is?" is no. Starfleet does have beacons in space that can tell starships the time, but try strapping one of those on.

But I say, "So what?" There are higher priorities in life. As long as you take the time to do things right, give yourself a little time to enjoy whatever planet you're on, have enough time for others, and treat the time you have as precious. Who really needs a Rolex?

Whatever else you may think of him, Soran had one good idea: if you carry a timepiece...keep it attached to you.

Elliott Marks

In *Star Trek Generations,* the first movie to feature the cast of *The Next Generation,* something terrible happens. No, not that. Something really terrible: the media shows up.

The 23rd-century descendants of today's TV and print reporters hound Kirk around the bridge of the *Enterprise-*B, taking time out, no doubt, from rehashing the O.J. trial. They pursue him for meaningless sound bites and colorful images, all the while sticking cameras and lights in his face.

Then they get lucky. A disaster takes place on board. Kirk is lost. What great news for the reporters.

When I was growing up, a question would occasionally be asked of newspaper publishers. Why is the paper filled with death and tragedy? Why is a murder always a headline? Why isn't there more positive news on the front page?

OK, that's more than one question, but you know what I mean. Occasionally some publisher or editor would answer. Inevitably they said something like this—"People aren't interested in a story about a plane making a safe landing. People won't buy a paper that features good news." These comments would always conclude that this was very sad but that was the way it was. Good news doesn't sell.

Later in my adult years, a new newspaper was introduced. You've heard of it: *USA Today.* The philosophy of this paper was to be colorful, upbeat, and positive. For the most part, murder and dirty laundry were kept off the front page.

Guess what? It sells like crazy. *USA Today* is the best-selling newspaper in America. People like positive news. They love to hear good things. And they'll pay good money to read about them.

I imagine this would make Gene Roddenberry smile. Although the majority of the media still embraces the negative, there is at least one vision of a better humanity. Darn good sports page, too.

I've never seen a newspaper on *Star Trek,* but I have a hunch that if we see a crew member reading one, it would be a descendent of *USA Today.* Because in the 24th century, man will be good, kind, and just—even the media.

In our office there's a woman who gets a phone call every afternoon at about 3:30. I've never been privy to these calls, but I know exactly whom they are from and what they are about. I've deduced all this information by overhearing a single phrase she utters into the telephone. "No fighting," she says. "No fighting!"

My brother Mark and I heard this precise phrase over the phone from our working mother countless times. Whenever it's half past three, it's a safe bet that somebody's mom is yelling these exact words into a phone somewhere.

My mother's solution was to make us stop calling. The fighting continued unabated for years, but at least she was spared.

Now this is going to sound like sour grapes, but it's

not. See, Mom always punished me for these battles. To her, it was simple. I was older, so I got punished.

"You should know better," she would say. As my bratty brother watched and smiled, I would trundle off to my room to serve my sentence. Of course, this made me angrier, and the following day at 3:30, I would knock that grin off Mark's face.

Years later I worked as a creative director at a small, family-run ad agency. Big mistake. The principals of the shop showed up only a couple of times a week. While they were away, I was responsible for directing the creative department to develop certain ads. When the principals returned, they would reclaim the power delegated to me and change everything. Soon my staff ignored virtually any direction I gave. This would only make me angrier and the following week I would take it out of Mark's hide. Oops.

What I mean is, over time I came to understand that both these situations were exactly the same. In both circumstances I was given responsibility but no authority. Big difference.

With Mark, I was responsible for preventing the fighting but had no mechanism to enforce my will. I couldn't tell him what to do. The only way I could make him listen was by beating him up. Not the recommended way to prevent fighting.

At the agency, I was responsible for directing the creative department but had no authority to enforce my will. The authority was usurped the second the principals showed up on the scene. My employees could just wait for their arrival and ignore me completely. Not the recommended way to get a team working for you.

Responsibility will produce results only when backed by authority. No one had to teach Picard that lesson.

While commanding a fleet protecting the Klingon border in "Redemption Part II," Picard orders his ships to reposition. One of his ship commanders, Data, disobeys this direct order.

Unknown to Picard, Data had figured a way to detect Romulan blockade runners. If he were to reposition as commanded, the Romulans would cross undetected. Instead, Data ignored the order and exposed the Romulans.

Picard could have court-martialed Data for disobedience. Instead he supported Data's decision. After all, he was the man who gave Data the responsibility of protecting the border, and the android's action prevented the Romulans from tipping the odds the wrong way. He gave Data both responsibility and authority. The result? No fighting.

My mom once spiced up a vacation to Nova Scotia by rolling my sister's car down an eleven-foot embankment. I couldn't watch. I was in the back seat of the car with my eyes closed. For a moment, time stopped and I felt myself straddle the line between life and death. Everyone survived but we were pretty badly shaken (especially my sister).

After filing the appropriate reports with the Royal Canadian Mounted Police, Mom and Dad took us all to a movie. They figured watching a film would take our minds off the accident. The movie was *The Sound of Music*. Sitting through *The Sound of Music* was worse than rolling down a cliff in a Chevy.

I was sixteen at the time and had never considered my own mortality. Suddenly it occupied the front of my mind, not far from the small lump on my forehead.

I began to think about what it should say on my tombstone. "How's it going?" is what I settled on. I figured there's some guy who cuts the grass in the cemetery and occasionally he looks at the headstones. When he looked at mine, he would mentally answer my question, How's it going? Hopefully he will think, "Fine."

That appeals to me because even though I would be dead, I would still be making people think. That would be a fine legacy.

On further reflection I've decided to be buried on the Genesis Planet. You know, so I could come back. I mean, who wouldn't prefer *Star Trek*'s take on life after death? People not only attain the afterlife. After they embrace the light, they return to their old jobs with death proving nothing more than an inconvenience. Hell, I've had paper cuts that interrupted my life more dramatically than the average fatality on *Star Trek*.

But Nova Scotia was very real. Except for an incident that I'm not sure actually happened. Let me explain.

After the Von Trapp family escaped from the nasty Nazis, we returned to our campsite and I took a shower. I washed out the last little piece of glass from my sister's Camaro. And I heard a voice. It said, "David."

The voice was close, next to me. I peered out the door, and no one was near. I couldn't tell if it was a man or woman who called me. Someone did. But I know that no one was there.

Perhaps *Star Trek* is closer to the truth than we think. At the line between mortality and beyond, our preconceptions break down. Anything is possible. Maybe even going and coming back. All I know is that next time I straddle that line, I want find out who that voice belongs to.

A BRIEF STOPOVER AT DEEP SPACE NINE

BENJAMIN SISKO

Not your average commanding officer:
Captain Benjamin L. Sisko (Avery Brooks).

Robbie Robinson

Benjamin Sisko is a different kind of commander. Not just because his command, Deep Space 9, doesn't fly around like a starship. It's because he's a dad. A pretty good one, too.

When I watch Ben and his son Jake, I wonder how my dad and I would have fared out by Bajor. Our relationship has always been somewhat rocky, but we've fared better than most father-and-son relationships portrayed in *Star Trek.*

Heck, the majority of *Star Trek* fatherhoods are a disaster from Kirk and David, to Spock and Sarek, to Worf and Alexander, to Riker and his dad. Picard became a surrogate father for a single episode ("Suddenly Human") and his surrogate kid stabbed him. The *Enterprise* could be the poster ship for dysfunctional families.

Well, relationships are hard to maintain, whether they're between fathers and sons or siblings or friends. Relationships demand work to stay strong. Bonds between people decay if they're not taken care of.

When I was a kid, my family crossed the George Washington Bridge on the way to visit relatives in New Jersey. As I looked up one of the towers, I noticed workers and said something brilliant like, "Hey, look at the painters." Necks immediately craned to view the workmen high over our heads. We were amazed. Then my father said something even more amazing—it was even possibly true.

"Those painters never finish painting the bridge," he said. "By the time they get to the other side they have to go back and start over again." *Wow,* I thought as I imagined those painters going to the George Washington Bridge every single day and never finishing the job. It's an image that has stayed with me for a lifetime.

I have come to see relationships the same way. You never stop taking care of them. To keep them fresh and beautiful, they require work. And the work lasts a lifetime.

Jake Sisko (Cirroc Lofton) and his father understand the importance of making time for the things that really matter.

Robbie Robinson

The strange thing is, *Star Trek: The Next Generation* outlasted the average American marriage. The show was on for seven years. Half the people who vow to love and cherish each other for all eternity call it quits in less time.

Still, there's a great role model out there. Way out there, on Deep Space 9, it's Benjamin Sisko. No matter how grave the crisis he faces, he makes his son a priority. Their relationship may be the strongest of any we've seen in the *Star Trek* universe.

They share the ups and downs of their lives together.

Ben can't always be there when Jake needs help with his homework, but he tries. He makes time for small things like a game of catch. And they plan wonderful adventures together. They even went on a 24th-century version of *Kon-Tiki* in the episode "Explorers."

They care about each other, and they work at it. An amazingly simple formula when you think about it. Consider the people you care about. Set time aside for them. Do stuff together. It can't be as hard as dragging a bucket of paint up the towers of the George Washington Bridge every day.

QUARK

Quark is a Ferengi. The Ferengi are the greediest species in the universe, with one exception: major-league baseball players.

What was that all about? The major-league baseball strike, I mean. O.K. we're making seven million dollars a year plus meal money. So let's go on strike. What? Well, Rule of Acquisition 97 states: " Enough...is never enough."

My goodness, these guys get to play baseball for a living. They should be having fun. How did they ever lose so much perspective?

Wait a minute. Maybe it's a glove thing. You know, Michael Jackson didn't get really weird until he started wearing a glove on one hand. And who else wears a glove on one hand? Baseball players. It's simple: The players, all wearing one glove like the King of Pop, mistakenly believed they should be paid as much as His Jacksonness. Then again, maybe they're just greedy.

Which makes them just like Quark. Well, not exactly just like him. Quark is smart, devious, and effective.

He also has one surprising characteristic: He is charming. But please, don't be fooled by his charm. Dracula was also one charming son of a devil.

Like a funhouse mirror, Quark (Armin Shimerman) humorously shows us how humans *shouldn't* be.

Robbie Robinson

Quark is the embodiment of greed. Everything is secondary to profit. His life is guided by a set of principles called the Rules of Acquisition. It drives me crazy when I overhear a kid reciting one of these rules.

No one should use this Ferengi as a role model no matter how sympathetically he is portrayed on the show. The actions of the species are despicable. Take how they view and treat women. To call their females second-class citizens is to elevate them in Ferengi society. Ferengi don't just keep their women barefoot and pregnant. They don't let them wear any clothes.

All their interpersonal relationships are meaningless compared to profit. Quark's own brother tried to trap him in an open airlock to take over control of his holdings. Quark complimented his brother on the attempt. Murdering your own family is perfectly acceptable behavior for a Ferengi.

If there's a single good thing that can be learned from this species, it's this. Likability is vastly overrated. The Ferengi homeworld is an entire planet of Eddie Haskells, capable of the expression of politeness but not its substance.

That said, I will spring to the defense of Quark's brother Rom and his nephew Nog. Both have shown flashes of some fine qualities: friendship, caring, respect. So perhaps there is some hope for the species after all.

You know, the quark is one of the smallest particles ever discovered by man. In my opinion, its namesake is just as small.

Sincerity is the most important thing. Once you can fake that, the rest is easy.

I've heard that remark attributed to George Burns and Bill Clinton, but I know another who could have uttered it. That big-lobed casino owner, Quark.

See, I think there's more to Quark then greed. There's also insincerity. Ah heck, this isn't a political campaign, so I'll just pull a William Safire. Quark is a congenital liar.

Everything that humans should be, he isn't. In fact, though profit resides at the center of his existence, he isn't even a very good businessman.

Let me show you why. He often deflects criticism of his actions with a phrase like, "It's just business—nothing personal." This is a terrible business position. Exactly the opposite is true. All business is personal.

In my profession, advertising, we compete with other ad agencies to gain new accounts. Usually a prospective client will draw up a document that says what resources and capabilities are desired. The document is called a Referral for Proposal, or RFP for short.

Our agency received one recently. Without divulging the company, here's what the RFP said. Triple X Corporation is looking for an advertising agency with over ten million dollars worth of billing. The agency must be full-service, containing creative, media, and account-service departments. A public relations unit is a plus. They would prefer their account to be one of the two largest accounts in the shop they choose. Experience with younger audiences, especially teens, is critical. And, of course, the agency and client should have the proper chemistry.

Chemistry. You know, like Bogart and Bacall, like sodium and chloride. Sure they were interested in our capabilities. *But* they also wanted chemistry. They wanted to see if they liked us.

What?!? Who cares if they like ya? Business is not a popularity contest.

Think not? Take a look at the flip side. Who wants to spend their time hanging around with jerks? Do you want to show up at work every day and sit across from someone who turns your stomach? Not me. Who cares how good they are at their job? Life is too short and the time we spend at work is too long to hang out with some obnoxious dweeb.

When you work with people you like, you're more productive. The personalities of your coworkers are important. Can you trust them? Do you respect them? Do you have chemistry? The search committee from Triple X Corporation had it right.

Why do you think Wal-Mart has greeters? Why do waitresses ask you if you're enjoying your meal? Why does IBM have a public relations department? Chemistry, that's why.

Ask yourself this: Do you stop at the nearest gas station or the one where they treat you like a friend, the one where you know somebody? I have two convenience stores within a half block of my front door. I always go to the same one. The one where there's chemistry. (It's also the one where I can run a tab.)

So I say this to Quark. All business is personal because business is conducted between people. And anyone who doesn't understand that is a very poor businessman indeed.

BACK ABOARD THE ENTERPRISE-D...

Perhaps the most important lesson I've learned during my four decades on this planet is to always put my keys in the same place.

No joke. When I misplace my keys, my life comes apart. I've been late to business meetings, irritated dates, even missed a flight to Nashville because I couldn't leave home without the means to get back inside. Fact is, I constantly mislay my keys.

I don't know how this can happen. I always leave my keys in the identical place, near the couch in plain view. It's easy. I come home, collapse on the couch, empty my pockets, and pick up the remote control. Hence, my keys are always in the same location. Until I need them.

Perhaps keys are migratory, heading south for the winter after the autumn solstice. Then there's the poltergeist theory. Or maybe it's just that I shouldn't have bought that Mexican Jumping Bean key chain.

On the up side, losing my keys is great exercise. I bound around the house, checking pants pockets, lifting and moving piles of stuff, retracing my steps, throwing my hands up in the air, bending over to look under the chairs....

Hey, wait a minute. With all the junk sports in the Olympics, this could become a big event. They could even put the competitors in bikinis, throw a little sand around the apartment, and call it Olympic Beach Key Finding. A ratings winner for sure.

Of course, on *Star Trek* they never lose a thing. I think Dr. McCoy might have misplaced a communicator once, but none of the crew of the *Enterprise*-D has ever exhibited such carelessness. You'd think they would. Communicators and phasers are that perfect losing size, as are most of the instruments that Drs. Crusher and Pulaski handle.

But we never see crew members ransacking their rooms looking for a lost anything. Is there some 24th-century invention that has solved this 20th-century epidemic?

I mean, sometimes I walk into a room looking for something and then I can't remember why I walked into the room. So I not only lose what I was looking for, I lose my train of thought. Not surprising, because it doesn't take much to derail that train.

If *The Next Generation* has a solution, I need it now. I also regularly lose my wallet, my checkbook, and my credit cards. Sometimes I'll leave my car at work and the next morning walk out the back door of my home and think someone has stolen my car. Once I lost my American Express card and later, after I had canceled it, found the card in my wallet.

My mom used to say that you always found something in the last place you looked for it. Wonderful folk wisdom but not any help. In reality, I know the only person that can solve this problem for me is me. Even if *Star Trek* had a device that could keep track of the things I lose, I'm convinced what I'd do with it. I'd lose it.

A recent assignment for our agency was to redesign a logo. Ad agencies are often given this task. Usually we're not so good at it.

People confuse designers, who work on logos and such, with art directors, who mostly conceive and lay out ads. They're easy to confuse. Both wear trendy clothes and indulge stylish tastes. They frequent foreign films and sushi bars. But the subtle difference in their talents belies the specialization of their expertise.

It is not unlike the difference between the scarlet king snake and the coral snake: They are virtually indistinguishable, with the small exception that one is highly poisonous. The deadly one has white rings around its red and black stripes. Wait. Maybe it has black rings on the outside of the white and red stripes. Or is that the harmless one? I never can remember.

Anyway, one should figure it out before heading into the woods.

The point is that people confuse the strengths of art directors and designers. Even art directors and designers make this error. And this leads to ad agencies being asked to design logos. Which, even though we're the wrong guys to ask, we will gladly do for a price. *Comprende?*

Naturally, I based our work on the best logo we could find. The one on the chests of the crew of the *Enterprise*-D. The Starfleet logo has all the characteristics for successful corporate communication.

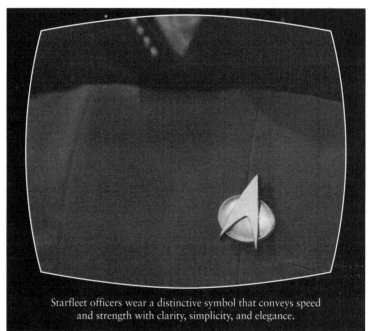

Starfleet officers wear a distinctive symbol that conveys speed
and strength with clarity, simplicity, and elegance.

One, it does the primary job of identifying the organization. The upward pointing "V" shape brings to mind the leading point of a starship. The underlying circle resembles a planet. Together they are distinctive and recognizable.

The logo conveys an attitude. Sleek lines and polished metal communicate speed and strength.

Change its size and put it on the cover of a manual or a computer screen and it stays recognizable, so it works in a variety of sizes and retains its identity even when rendered in a single color.

Totally amazing. An episode of *Star Trek: The Next Generation* may be equivalent to a year at a school of design. The tuition is less, too.

Using the *Star Trek* design criteria, we created a number of logos for our client. They chose one. You've probably seen it. I think it's pretty good. (You'll forgive me if don't reveal the logo; I prefer to let the client continue to think that our brilliant design was inspired by their input, not outer space.)

Sometimes ad agencies are asked to design logos. Usually we're not so good at it. But occasionally with a little help from our friends at Starfleet, we do just fine, thank you.

Time is relative. As a kid, I remember that the last two weeks of school before summer vacation seemed to take years. Now an entire summer flashes by before I'm able to put on my swim trunks.

It makes sense. To a five-year-old, a year is 20% of his life. To a twenty-year-old, that same year is only 5% of her life. At fifty that year has shrunk to 2%.

My hypothesis is that a fifty-year-old senses a year of time the same way a five-year-old senses a month. The older you get, the faster you perceive time as moving.

But every now and again, no matter what your age, time stands still. Intensity freezes moments, and while we're in those moments, they last forever.

Taking off from Miami in a small airplane a few years ago, I experienced such a moment. As we accelerated down the runway, the plane suddenly shuddered. The brakes squealed. I looked at my traveling companion and said, "This ain't good." And then nothing happened. The most wonderful nothing imaginable. The plane stopped without incident.

Birds had flown across the runway and the captain decided to let them clear the area. After braking, he returned to the takeoff point and we did it again. Uneventfully.

I've replayed this moment many times. As scary as it was, there was a gift in there. It showed me why a placid man like Picard and a thrill seeker like Riker wanted to be in the same place. It demonstrated to me why the crew of the *Enterprise*-D is on that ship. It reminded me why I had taken up skydiving.

To be in an unknown or uncertain position is interesting. Interesting may not be a strong enough word, but it is the right idea. We need to be shaken out of our everyday lives from time to time.

The *Enterprise*-D is as much a vehicle of self-discovery as it is of space exploration. It breaks open complacency. Introduces the unexpected. In those moments the wheel of life is spinning. In those moments we live forever:

When the *Enterprise* is doomed. When the warp core is about to explode. When the ship is outgunned. When the plane wheels are squealing on the runway in Miami. These are powerful stimulants. They outweigh the passage of time. And they help us appreciate the temporal nature of our lives.

If I sound like I'm endorsing life as an adrenaline junkie—I'm not. I'm saying time is relative. You can speed it up, slow it down, or just watch it pass by. Time is your own, whether you're five or fifty. The folks on the bridge of the *Enterprise*-D are squeezing every drop out of it. They remind us of what we can do with time. It's time to choose.

The other day I received a simple request: Accelerate the timetable of a voice-over session to achieve an earlier completion date for a commercial. A minor problem existed with the new schedule: It was impossible to meet.

If *Star Trek* teaches us anything, it is that the impossible is attainable. In this case, however, my chances of beating the deadline were as likely as a Klingon turning the other cheek.

See, the script for the announcer was not finished. Ergo we could not record his voice. I suppose we could have recorded all the words in the English language and then edited them together to match the final script. But then the commercial would have sounded like the telephone computer voice that spits out phone numbers when you call information. And I hate the way that computer sounds, don't you?

No, this request was impossible to meet. An alternate date for completion would have to be negotiated. Sitting down with the appropriate agency members we set a new date, two weeks later than the clients had requested. Now we had to break the news to them.

The final issue to be dealt with was, should we act like Montgomery Scott or Geordi La Forge? In the episode "Relics," these two brilliant engineers discussed timetables.

Scotty inflates his estimates by a factor of four. This allows him to beat the schedule and be perceived as a miracle worker. Geordi gives an accurate estimate and hopes to complete the work on time.

In "Phantasms," La Forge's honest assessments embarrass him as factors beyond his control ruin his projections. Every time he tells the captain that the warp engines are ready to come on-line, they break down and he needs more time. Not a good day.

Scotty with his built-in time cushion would not have suffered the same fate. Using the Scotty method, we could promise a delivery date three weeks out. Then if we could meet our internal deadline of two weeks, we would exceed the client's expectations.

Alas, when it came time to revise the schedule for the voiceover, we choose the La Forge method. Because as wonderful as it is to be a miracle worker, we were more comfortable with the truth. Somebody once said, "It's easier to tell the truth because you don't have to remember as much." That body is right.

But more importantly, we owe honesty to the folks who pay our salaries. And if you can't achieve the impossible, the least they deserve is to know the truth. I'm sure Geordi would agree.

Every year I try something new. This year I'm taking golf lessons. Golf is the perfect sport for old, slow, white guys like me, especially if you use a cart.

Mark Twain called golf a good walk spoiled. George Carlin considers it an elitist sport that wastes entirely too much land. They're both right. Still, I'm having fun learning to play.

It's a silly game, hitting a tiny ball hundreds of yards toward a hole so small that it needs a flag stuck in it so the golfers can see it. Fifteen separate clubs composited from the world's most expensive alloys are required to accomplish this task. Golf balls are covered with dimple patterns based on aerodynamic flow. An agricultural industry has developed around blending grasses to produce the perfect fairway. Thousands of books, videos, and gadgets are dedicated to the development of the perfect golf swing. None of it works.

Golf's chief attraction—at least for me—is that the game requires no opponent. You can play against others if you like, but you can play with them too. It doesn't matter, because every game is just you against the golf course.

Problematically, it eliminates the possibility of blaming anyone but yourself for your horrible score. I've noticed this doesn't stop the players from blaming everything except themselves. They "didn't hit the putt too hard, the groundskeeper didn't water the greens enough. Besides, the lip on the hole is too high." Or "the birds sang too loudly" during their backswing. I've actually heard a playing partner say that his magnificent stroke was ruined because some idiot put a lake in the wrong spot. Golfers complain more than a Ferengi with an earache.

I've tried to avoid this fault. Complainers are big babies. Complaining accomplishes nothing. It is noticeably lacking on the bridge of the *Enterprise*-D.

This is an example for us all to follow. The worse the situation on the *Enterprise,* the more the crew buckles down and takes responsibility for its own actions.

Geordi never cries out, "Data made me do it." Riker never rolls his eyes and whines about a Picard decision. Troi never gripes that a bird chirped during her backswing.

Complaining is wasted energy. Criticism and dissent have their place, but don't confuse them with grousing. They never do it on the *Enterprise*-D. I try not to do it in life. I even try on the golf course.

And another thing. What's this business about conquering space? You hear it from time to time. Somebody says, "If we can conquer space why can't we conquer…whatever?"

Listen. We have *not* conquered space. We put some folks in orbit, landed a few guys on the moon, sent probes to a couple of planets. Let's not get carried away here. This is not conquering.

The Milky Way Galaxy is a hundred thousand light-years across. All our space achievements have taken place inside of a few light-hours.

We're still in the get-acquainted period.

Put it another way. You take your kid to the beach.

He wades in up to his knees, splashes around a little, maybe fills a pail with water. The kid has not conquered the ocean. But he has conquered more of the ocean than mankind has conquered of our galaxy. And the Milky Way is just a tiny little part of space. The whole is really, really big.

During *The Original Series,* the Federation had only explored a small fraction of the galaxy, not unlike the Vikings exploring the Atlantic. The *Enterprise*-D made a marginally larger dent. Yet even with only that small piece of space, it found diversity and phenomena beyond imagination. We will find much, much more.

Sure, *Star Trek* is fantasy. But the simple premise that mankind's future is in space is profound. And it's true.

Space becomes a larger part of our lives with each passing year. Our maps, our insulation, our strongest metals, our drugs, our everything are all more advanced—and, in many cases, made possible—because of the space program. As I sit here typing on my computer, I'm reminded that the microprocessor that runs it was transformed from an oddity into a powerful tool because it was needed in space capsules. Today, you can find microprocessors in the refrigerators and dishwashers of people who think space has nothing to do with their lives.

More importantly, we have nowhere else to go. Human population has exploded well past the point of being stopped, sans global catastrophe. Our finite resources are disappearing, along with millions of species. To my mind, the only meaningful result of recycling has been a proliferation of *Brady Bunch* movies. *Yikes!* It doesn't take an Albert Einstein to figure out that we have to figure something out.

Understand this: I'm not suggesting space is the answer to Man's problems. Man is the answer to Man's problems. But space is a necessary part of the solution. The things that drive us out into space are the noblest intents of humanity: the desire to learn, to explore, to understand. These are the qualities that a mature species will use to solve its problems.

Hey, we may never conquer space. But we have to try. Because if we turn our backs on space, we are turning away from the best part of ourselves.

Humans have a basic problem. We kill each other. This is no minor flaw. Our advancing technology magnifies this vice. A really angry caveman might have been able to whack a few fellow cavemen if they were close enough to hit with a stick. Today, one angry person with access to a nuclear weapon could whack millions. There might even be a way for a clever angry person to get us all. Pleasant thought, huh?

I guess the point, at this point, is that technology doesn't solve problems. Not the really fundamental human problems.

Take television. Twenty years ago there were three network channels and precious little else on the airwaves. A little over ten years ago cable gave us thirty choices. As the technology advanced, so did the number of channels we could get. Soon, to fill the void, numerous mindless programs sprang into existence. Now there's talk about systems that can deliver five hundred channels. Great, five hundred channels and nothing is on. Technology marches on...but to what end?

Here's something to think about. Our technological tools of agriculture allow us to produce enough food to feed everyone on the planet. *Everyone.* No one has to go to bed hungry. But tonight people will starve to death—*to death.* Technology is only as good—or as evil—as the hands that wield it.

Gene Roddenberry faced this problem when he created the world of the future. He wanted *Star Trek* to take place in a time when man had conquered war, conquered poverty, conquered hunger. And he knew that technology alone wouldn't do the job.

So the humans who populate the bridge of the *Starship Enterprise* are more evolved than the folks walking around today. Not physically—it's their humanity that is more evolved. They're a more rational, less aggressive brand of human.

It's why they're such good role models. The citizens

of the Federation show each other common decency and respect.

Yeah, I know, there's a lot of backsliding that goes on. For a leader of a nonaggressive species, Kirk got into a lot of fights. Bones McCoy seems to enjoy needling Mr. Spock. And even in the 24th century, Dr. Beverly Crusher is as irritating as humans come.

Still, when you compare how they treat each other to how people treat each other today, those guys are flat-out better than us. Which gives us something to aspire to.

Gene Roddenberry called contemporary humans an adolescent species. I agree. We're not only adolescent, we're juvenile delinquents. Juvenile delinquents who play with nuclear bombs. Let's hope we grow up soon.

My mother came from a family of eleven, and my father from a family of ten. Coming from such large families, they desired to have a small one. They decided to have only six children. Which they did.

It was easy to spot us. We were the kids that were wearing clothes a size too big or a size too small. Hand-me-downs were a way of life.

We didn't consider ourselves poor, but the eight of us

lived in a three-bedroom apartment. Mom, Dad, and the baby slept in my parents' room. My three sisters slept in another room. And my older brother and I shared the remaining bedroom. We all shared one bathroom. We were a close family whether we wanted to be or not.

From my vantage point in the middle of the family, it never seemed crowded. Maybe that's because by the time I came along, fourth-born, the place was already pretty full. Or maybe it was because we all found our own space. Our interests were different. Our friends were different. Our relationships to each other were different. We each found places inside and outside the family to call our own.

Of course, with that many people in such close proximity, differences popped up. My solution was simple. I would only fight with siblings younger than me, where my size advantage made me invincible. Until Dad got home.

As full as our house was, there were always other kids around when it was time for dinner. I guess when you're feeding eight, an extra mouth or two doesn't make much difference. Mom was always happy to set a plate for our friends. Maybe she was just happy to expand her small family into something closer to the size she grew up with.

Families with more than three members are unusual on *Star Trek*. There may be some, but none jump to mind. I don't know why. With all those new planets to colonize, you would think that families with lots of kids would be an advantage, the same way they were in Jamestown and Plymouth.

I hope this isn't an homage to some politically correct notion like zero population growth. Could be. But a spacefaring species that desires zero population will soon achieve that objective. No population.

I am a single man. I'm happy with the choices and the consequences of my life. But sometimes my thoughts travel the road I didn't take.

Jean-Luc Picard does the same thing while visiting the nexus in *Generations*. He experiences his heart's deepest desire. He is a father with many children on Christmas Day. Even for the cool, professional captain, the tug of family ties is strong.

Ultimately, when forced to make a choice, Picard picks his single life. Because that is who he really is. He loves his family, but he must be true to himself.

Not long ago, I ventured to the Marinaccio Family Reunion. I saw my aunts and uncles, nieces and nephews, in-laws and cousins. Felt the warmth and reassurance of a big family. It was great fun.

The reunion brought a flood of melancholy memories. I remembered the big family and the little apartment I grew up in. At the end of the day I headed home to my one-bedroom condo. And I felt great.

I love the space and freedom of being single. The choices I've made have given me an interesting life and filled it with love. I don't think I'll be single for the rest of my life. (The truth is that my bachelorhood is on the endangered species list.) But I wouldn't trade a minute of the 45 years I've stood alone on my own two feet. Like Jean-Luc, I'm very comfortable in the chair I sit in.

What about the laundry? Who does the laundry on *Star Trek?* I mean, look at those guys. Always clean and pressed. But I've never seen a hamper in any crew member's quarters. Speaking of quarters, I've never noticed a laundromat either. So who does the laundry?

And don't try that "24th-century fabrics don't get dirty" stuff with me. I've seen plenty of dirty clothes on *The Original Series* and *The Next Generation.* Picard stays cleaner than Kirk used to, but the crew of the *Enterprise-*D manages to get itself quite messy.

Back here in the 20th century, our lives are consumed with laundry. In America, each day produces another 170 million sets of dirty clothes, not to mention 340 million dirty socks. No wonder the grocery stores are filled with Tide.

Still, it took me years to understand that if I didn't wash my clothes, eventually I wouldn't have anything to wear to work.

I've come to realize that this is a defining moment in life — an important rite of passage from youth to adulthood. The dawn, it dawns on you, that you gotta clean your threads. The day there are more clean shirts in your closet than dirty ones on your floor, that is really the day a boy becomes a man.

Heck, I took my laundry home to my mother until I

was 24, even though I had lived away from home since I turned 19. You cannot cut the apron strings until you let go of the laundry bag.

Cut those and a string of questions appears. How many times can one wear a shirt before it must be washed? Two? Three? And what about trousers? Is it truly necessary to separate whites from colors? What, if any, is the reason for the hot and cold water dial? Does load size really make a difference? How much is too much detergent? What's better, powder or liquid? And most importantly, how close is the nearest dry cleaner?

This is intimidating stuff for young guys. I know, I used to be one. Luckily, I found the nearest dry cleaner. Lustere. Nice folks. Ninety-nine cents a shirt.

Now try this on for size. Possibly the reason we never see the folks who clean the soiled uniforms on the *Enterprise* is that the captain and crew prefer not to air their dirty laundry in public. And that is a wonderful example to follow.

A SHORT RENDEZVOUS WITH VOYAGER

JANEWAY

The commander of the *Starship Voyager*,
Captain Kathryn Janeway (Kate Mulgrew).

Robbie Robinson

I magine a transporter malfunction—the transporter is a finicky piece of equipment. Captain James T. Kirk is about to beam down to ancient earth. Accidentally, a 20th-century film star is in the beam.

What materializes is a combination of Kirk and actress Katharine Hepburn. What materializes is Kathryn Janeway, captain of the *Starship Voyager*.

This is a wonderful development. Two of my favorite things are Captain Kirk and Katharine Hepburn. The *Voyager* couldn't be in better hands. After all, wasn't it Hepburn who guided that boat through the rapids in *The African Queen?* Hepburn who battled men eye-to-eye in an era when women weren't supposed to be equals? They even have the same name, Kate.

Janeway's biggest challenge (bigger ones will be coming I'm sure) was to meld two crews, two different ideologies, into a unit. Forget the particulars. What enabled her to take control was the force of her personality.

Kathryn Janeway is always very clearly in charge. She commands her folks and she commands the Maquis. She makes the merger work.

This is substantially different from the way the London office of Needham, Harper & Steers, and that of Doyle, Dane, Bernbach were merged by an advertising agency president a few years ago. A larger worldwide merger of these companies had occurred. The British capital was one of the cities where the new entity, called DDB Needham, found itself with two offices.

Both London operations had high profiles and were populated by ambitious and talented people. In this situation there were many options. DDB could have been merged into Needham with Needham's management running the show or vice versa. Or a representative of the new worldwide entity could have shown up and picked the best people from both firms to manage the new place. They could have done anything

What the president of the new, improved, larger worldwide agency did was something amazing. I'm not making this up. He sent a fax to both offices informing them they would merge. A *fax!* Chaos ensued. Everyone fought for his or her little piece of territory. Cooperation between the two London offices ceased (if it had ever started) to exist.

Quite simply, no one knew who was in charge. A problem that never occurs on *Voyager*.

What the president of DDB Needham should have done was to have found Kate Hepburn and James T. Kirk, put them in a transporter, and combined them as they rematerialized in London. Trust me, the person stepping out of the transporter would have taken charge.

It's a simple lesson, really. When you're in the captain's chair, be the captain. Just like Kate.

BACK IN THE ALPHA QUADRANT...

When I was a young writer at J. Walter Thompson Advertising in Chicago, I hardly ever left the building. I would stick around after hours, finishing my own work, and prowl the halls to see who else was working late. When I saw the lights on in an office, I would walk in and ask if I could help. Many nights I slept in my office, washing my hair in the men's room sink in the morning. I learned a lot this way. I smelled a bit gamey, but I learned a lot.

In truth I had to roam the halls to find work. My boss had a low opinion of me, rarely trusting me to work on any juicy assignments. So I would go outside our group. Sometimes I would find people who were so swamped with assignments they didn't care where, or from whom, the help came. My first ads were produced this way.

Over time I began to get the reputation of a bright young writer. About the same time, my boss realized that I worked for him. Soon after, he charged me with carrying my share of our group's load.

No one ever confused me with a workaholic, but I spent an awful lot of time in those offices. I guess I never really considered it work.

The same is true on the *Enterprise*-D. I mean, these guys are working day and night under extremely stressful circumstances. Well, more than stressful. Often some creature is trying to eat them or take over the ship and turn the entire crew into half-robot/half-human slaves. In fact, if Starfleet didn't work overtime, Earth would surely be a burnt-out cinder by now.

Just watch them at their stations. It's easy to tell they love their jobs. The work is challenging. The standards are high. The boss is tough but positive. No wonder there's a spring in their steps.

Compare them with the Borg. Slow, joyless automatons that are obviously just waiting for five o'clock to punch out. There is a spring in their steps too. But it's an actual metal spring, the kind we used to use to keep screen doors closed. Where's the fun in that?

The commonality between my approach to the job and that of the crew of the *Enterprise*-D is that I never considered advertising to be work. I was amazed my bosses let me do it. I loved creating ads and television commercials. It was a fun challenge, like a game. And unlike on the *Enterprise*-D, there's no real danger at an advertising agency. About the worst it gets is when the coffee is a little cold. I can handle that.

I've stayed in the ad game all these years because I've never lost that sense of fun. Like the captain and crew

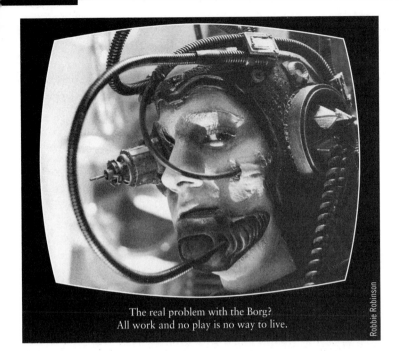

The real problem with the Borg?
All work and no play is no way to live.

Robbie Robinson

of the *Enterprise*-D, I don't consider it to be work. And that's the real secret of making a living. Find a job you love and you'll never work a day in your life.

I shot a television commercial on a dry lake bed in the high desert of California during August. Every day the temperature would hover around 95 degrees, and then the sun would come up.

We were armed with a water truck, gallons of sports drink, tents for shade, hats, sunscreen, and Ray-Bans. We avoided the hottest part of the day, quitting work between 11 A.M. and resuming at 3 P.M. We kept car air conditioners on full and retreated into the cool continuously. But we were no match for the average-sized star just over 90 million miles away.

By the end of the shoot we were shot. Our machinery had broken down. But our civility never did. We persevered.

The previous January, I shot a television commercial in Miami. The shooting was uneventful. By that I mean it went well. However, while we worked at the southern tip of Florida, our coworkers in DC got blasted by a blizzard. As the East Coast airports unfroze, I flew home. It was a week after the storm hit, and the city was still a mess. Any city without a federal government located in it probably would have been cleared; nonetheless, I trudged through the final snowbanks to my front door.

These encounters with the extremes of weather proved little more than inconveniences. But in a small way they illustrate the point I'm about to make. The earth is a hostile environment. In many ways more inhospitable to human life than space is.

Whoa, Dave. That's quite a leap you've taken there. More hostile than space? Space is a vacuum. There's no air. Its temperature is three degrees above absolute zero.

Sure, there are dangers in space, but let's take a second

look at our own home. Every year people on the earth are attacked by tornadoes, hurricanes, earthquakes, volcanoes, tidal waves, and firestorms. Even space contributes to the havoc, raining meteorites through the atmosphere.

The greatest threat to humanity is the earth itself. Early in the history of life on this planet, natural forces created a gas that killed over 90% of the then-living species. Of course this was good news for us; the gas was oxygen. Since then millions more species have gone extinct. The earth has been horrible to the lifeforms that arose on it. What we call the balance of nature is really one catastrophic event after another with little rhyme or reason.

If humans blew up the entire planet tomorrow, we wouldn't cause a fraction of the extinctions that the earth has in its history. Worse, it is only a matter of time before the earth changes, with or without our help, into a place uninhabitable to people. Someday Earth will get us.

Space, while not marvelously benign, seems to be a more stable environment. Tough place to live, for sure, but dependable.

If, like those on the *Enterprise,* we use our technology to make space our homes, it may prove less hostile than living on a planetary surface. Hey, we at least owe it to ourselves to check it out.

Living in space will probably turn out to be a bit harder than hanging around the captain's ready room drinking Earl Grey tea. But from what I've seen of space shuttle missions, it might be easier than melting on a dry lake bed in August.

I left my coffee in the microwave a little too long a couple of days ago. It came out bubbling. Since the entire process took forty seconds and I witnessed the event, it destroyed a cliché that my mother had taught me years before: "A watched pot never boils."

Nowadays, modern technology can supersede the wisdom of the ages. Let's face it. Watched pots boil all the time. A penny saved is a waste of space. Sorry.

These obsolete expressions are the result of a greater truth. Most of my life, and yours, is unimaginable to those who came before. At the turn of the century, cars were a rarity. Within fifty years they were a necessity. The computer on which I'm typing didn't exist thirty years ago. Tomorrow, grade schoolers will begin their days by booting up and surfing the Web. Soon those PCs will be as ancient as eggbeaters.

None of this, however, will affect the crew of the *Enterprise*. Because one of the remarkable things about *Star Trek*—in fact the thing I'm about to remark on—is their remarks. Or, more precisely, the remarks they don't make. They rarely use adages.

Even when they do use a cliché, it really isn't a part of speech. First they reference the source. Some phrase like, "As the Klingons say," will set up a maxim: "Revenge is a dish best served cold."

That's not really using a cliché so much as quoting one. Speaking of Klingons, the one great cliché user in *Star Trek* history came from their empire: General Chang (from *Star Trek VI: The Undiscovered Country*). And he was a jerk. 'Nuff said.

I rather like the way they use language on *Star Trek*. It's somewhat formal and touched with politeness. Even lowbrow conversations in Quark's bar have a highbrow sound to them. In fact, next time you watch, listen to the quiet of the shows. There's a calmness to Miles O'Brien's melodious tones, to Julian Bashir's utterances. Even half-Klingon B'Elanna Torres speaks softly. Of course, don't forget that she carries a big phaser.

At any rate, I believe the language on *Star Trek* promotes civility. It would have been hard to stay so dignified in my home growing up. We substituted yelling for talking. There was a certain passion to our communication, but most of us have poor hearing as adults. Think it's related?

We were more like *The Original Series*. You know, McCoy had a way of making everything an emergency. "Dammit Spock, pass the salt shaker. I need it." Oh well.

So as we move toward the millennium, I hope we are moving toward the tone of *The Next Generation*. Although that's probably too much to hope for. What will probably happen is new clichés will sneak into our speech, replacing the ones that are no longer relevant. I do know for certain that a watched fax never prints.

Gene Roddenberry dreamed of a species in which the members treated each other with common decency and respect, where the best instincts ruled a peaceful society, where murder was an incomprehensible occurrence.

There is such a species, but we don't have to travel light-years into space or centuries into Roddenberry's vision of the future to find them. They're here on earth. They're simians.

You know—apes. Let's take a good long look at gorillas. They're less greedy than Ferengi. More cuddly than Klingons. Less devious than Romulans. More loving than Vulcans. And less self-destructive than human beings. Their failings are few, their virtues many.

I'm not joking about this. Watching television the other night (as I'm prone to do. Well, not actually prone. Just sort of sitting back with my feet up), I saw something amazing.

A small boy had fallen into the gorilla enclosure at a zoo near Chicago. The tumble left him helpless and unconscious on the concrete floor of the exhibit. This is a true story. You can watch it yourself because someone videotaped the whole thing.

As the child lay helpless, a female gorilla walked over to him, picked him up, and brought him to the door where zookeepers could enter the cage. And while she patiently waited for humans to retrieve the injured boy, she caressed him, lovingly hugged him. It's touching to watch.

I lived in Chicago. I loved it. It's a great city. But there are parts of that toddlin' town where that child wouldn't have fared nearly as well. When I lived there, I saw a news report about a newborn baby that had been thrown away, tossed into a Dumpster. It isn't just the Windy City. Similar atrocities occur in cities all over this planet.

We could all learn something from that gorilla. Watching her, I mused that the word *humane* should be changed to *simiane*. Better still, rename Earth; call it the Planet of the Apes.

OK, I'm overboard again. But if mankind is able to achieve the peaceful status imagined by Roddenberry, we will have to admit that one of our greatest faults is arrogance. We should realize that while we are the dominant species on the planet, we are not best in all ways. There are superior species, or at least species who exhibit behavior superior to ours, right here at home. Any truly advanced species should be humble enough to learn from them. If we do that, then certainly our best days are in front of us.

I recently saw *Star Trek: First Contact*. As each new incarnation of Gene Roddenberry's creation appears, it reminds me of my affection for *The Original Series*. While the *Star Trek* of Kirk and Spock lacked the polish of *The Next Generation* or *Deep Space Nine* or *Voyager*, for me that was part of the fun. Besides, we were lucky to have *Star Trek* at all.

Back in 1966 there were tremendous problems producing the series. Creating new worlds every week was a strain on the people making the show. As needs arose, they came up with solutions on the fly. Some worked, others were ridiculous. I mean, did anyone buy that McCoy could animate Spock's brainless body with the remote control from a toy car? How about the entire population of Gideon dressing in leftover sperm costumes from Woody Allen's *Everything You Ever Wanted to Know About Sex But Were Afraid to Ask*? Talk about your cheesy costumes—my brother Mark once described the Horta as a moving slice of pizza.

Even a casual observer could notice the same sets and materials were being used over and over again. Every other episode gave me déjà vu. Hell, they were even recycling the actors. Die in this episode. Come back later as a different character. (Spock's father Sarek started out this way as a Romulan.)

Better funding for *The Next Generation* settled most of these problems. Special effects were improved tremendously. The look and feel of the show was more like the future. Oh, there were still the occasional inconsistencies, but on the whole the shows held together much better.

The acting was also more restrained. Gone were the days of chewing up the wallpaper whenever danger reared its ugly head.

So in terms of production and performances, *The Next Generation* was clearly superior. Which probably explains why I prefer *The Original Series*.

Kirk's *Star Trek* was like Lindbergh's flight across the Atlantic in the *Spirit of St. Louis*. Nobody had done anything like it before. Both were pioneers that fired the imagination.

Comparably, *The Next Generation* was like crossing the Atlantic in a 747. It was bigger, more expensive, smoother, and more comfortable. And it was still wonderful to cross the ocean. But I missed the bumpy, often outrageous ride.

Hey, so what if Kirk digested a little wallpaper? He was racing all over the galaxy at warp 9, his ship about to explode, the phasers off-line, facing certain death at the hands—or corresponding anatomical feature—of some unknown alien. He couldn't possibly overreact (or overact) considering the circumstances. In such dire circumstances the only reasonable action to take is to eat the wallpaper and then start munching on the secondary hull.

Besides, without Kirk, Spock, and McCoy, there'd be no Picard, Riker, and Data. The concepts that make *Star Trek* go were all invented in the original: the Prime Directive, the respect and decency the crew members show each other, the Federation, the mission, the bravery to deal with subjects like racism, overpopulation, and man's place in a technological society—the everything.

Don't get me wrong; I love *The Next Generation*. Many of my favorite *Star Trek* moments have taken place on the *Enterprise*-D and -E. But let's face it, I'm an old dude. *The Original Series* is *my* generation.

One thing does bother me, though. Shouldn't the 24th century have a starship named the *U.S.S. Kirk?* There are ships named after Hood and Farragut and Grissom. I think there should have been a *Starship Kirk* within fifteen minutes of James T.'s trip through the hole in the hull of the *Enterprise*-B.

He is the single most important person in the *Star Trek* universe. He's saved the galaxy more often than most folks go to Circle K. It is time to rectify this tremendous oversight. I think it would be poetic justice to rename the *Excelsior*—taking the very ship that was sent to hunt him down as a renegade — and give it his name. At any rate I hope to see the *U.S.S. Kirk* soon. Very soon.

In the end—and this is the end—I've learned a great deal from *Star Trek: The Next Generation*. In fact, I've gleaned insights from *every* incarnation of Gene Roddenberry's creation. That's not the amazing thing. The truly astonishing thing is that there is new *Star Trek* being created thirty years after we first saw the *Enterprise*.

As the legacy of *Star Trek* continues, *The Next Generation* will always hold a special place for me. The series made an important advance from its predecessor. *The Original Series* was big and bold. The good guys were good. The bad guys were bad. The morality play was performed in black and white. *The Next Generation* brought texture and shades of gray.

Gene Roddenberry has been quoted as saying that the Klingons in *The Original Series* were never given enough depth. They were simply evil. He fixed that oversimplification in *The Next Generation*. In 1987, he put Worf on the bridge of the *Enterprise*-D. Through him we got to know the Klingons. We came to admire their nobility and to understand their savagery.

Worf also served as a symbol of one of *Star Trek*'s greatest lessons. That through understanding, conflict can be resolved. Prophetically, not long after it was shown that the Klingons and Federation had ceased hostilities, the United States and Soviet Union did the same. I'm not claiming cause and effect here; I just thought I'd mention it.

Over the course of *The Next Generation* we watched a more enlightened scenario play out. No longer were any species portrayed as totally good or evil. Even the Ferengi were given their shining moments.

The same was true of the exploration of individuals. Q, who appeared as the embodiment of arrogance, was found to be humorous and caring.

Lore, the evil twin of Data, wasn't simply evil. His character had depth and anguish, and maybe even achieved redemption.

The Crystalline Entity that had seemed a simple killing machine was shown to be a complex being with the ability to communicate.

Even the monomaniacal Borg showed redeeming qualities in the person of Hugh. If the Borg are pure evil, then they are less than the sum of their parts. Taken as individuals, even the Borg can be warm, loving friends.

This feature of *The Next Generation* elevated the show. To me, it is an expression as powerful as any *Star Trek* imagery. Indeed, it is a powerful philosophy to live by.

The phrase "Live long and prosper" has long been associated with *Star Trek*. I have come to believe that the lessons of *The Next Generation* can help you do just that. Not only for individuals like you and me, but for our species. For if we can find the good in everyone, we will live lives that are rich beyond measure.

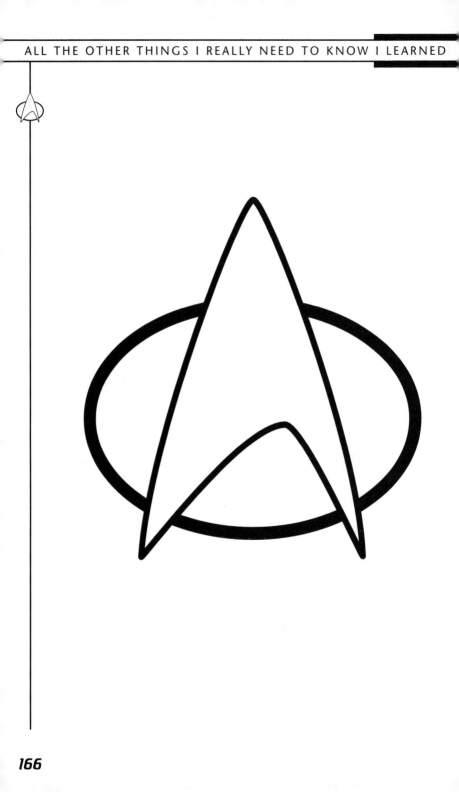

ACKNOWLEDGMENTS

*T*hanks to a lot of guys named Jim. A couple of guys named Mike. Tessa. Jane. Marco and Margaret. Justina, Timothy, Amber, Courteney, and Kurt Marinaccio. A bunch of other Marinaccios. Michael and Steven Brennen. Alan Bennett. Little and Barney. Paul, Chris, Andy, and Jerry. Muscos from Maine to Florida. All the folks at LM&O who don't bother me when my door is closed.